REVERSE TOMBOY

REVERSE
TOMBOY

A novel

Auto Anon

This novel is entirely a work of fiction. The names, characters and incidents portrayed in it are the work of the author's imagination. Any resemblance to actual persons, living or dead, events or localities is entirely coincidental.

ISBN 978-1-0694767-0-8

"If I Could Tell You" © 1940 W.H. Auden

"Musée des Beaux Arts" © 1938 W.H. Auden

Cover art by Remy Boydell

Auto Anon logo design by Max Schwartz

Frontispiece: *Seated Nude: Study for 'Une Baignade',* 1884, Georges Seurat, National Gallery, London.

Contents

Author's Foreword   i

Part One: Swimming Forward   3

Part Two: Treading Water   29

Part Three: Epilogue   70

Part Four: Poems   75

Part Five: Trans Femme Masculinity, What Do We Want?   99

To Nancy Richler, I'm sorry I couldn't keep my promise.

To Phil Hall, for inviting me to so many literary events I had no business attending.

And to Kathrin Hemingway, who never published under this name which she chose for herself during her 1953 holiday with her wife Mary.

Author's Foreword

I am not sure if this is a modest book, but I am a modest author. There was a time when I was very proud of the work you are about to read. But it was written over half a decade ago, and now I am detached from it enough that I no longer have that mercurial relationship to it I have to my fresher work. When a work is fresh, I tend to sway between an anxious fear that it is trash and an overly aggrandized hope for it. I am detached enough from this little book to not feel that anymore. I still very much hope that it is good, but that hope is more a hope that you will enjoy it and find it worthy your time. It means much less to me than it used to for it to be appraised as important or skillful. Although, I do have some reason to suspect that it is good. When I wrote it, I sent it out to one publisher, only one, and they wished to publish it. It was a small well-respected publisher, which will go unnamed, but very much of the sort that prided itself on publishing good work that progressed the voices of the marginalized.

Right after I received an email that my book had made the shortlist to be considered for publication, and that I would receive a follow up email in a bit informing me of if it had made the final cut, the Black Lives Matter protests began. I then received an email saying that unless I included more characters of colour that my book would not be published. At the time I was rather indignant about this, partly because about half of my characters were subtly hinted at being racialized, but I found writing descriptions of characters' 'ebony skin shinning in the moonlight' or whatever rather gauche and ghoulish. While that email told me they would reconsider my book if I edited it as they requested, I never did. I let it sit on a hard drive for half a decade instead. This is partly because the wind had left my sail, the momentum to publish it had been lost as other career opportunities came up. Somewhat ironically, the only major change I have made to the manuscript is the one that publisher requested, I have made the protagonist explicitly Jewish, and other racialized characters more obviously racialized. I hope that this change was for the better. I've convinced myself it was. Otherwise, what you are about to read, is unchanged from the original manuscript I submitted all those years ago. Instead of submitting it for publication again, I decided to self-publish it. The reason I have made this decision is simply because I feel too removed from the text to go through the traditional publishing process with it. It belongs not to me, but to a former me.

The trans literary scene has changed a lot in those five years. And the book you have before you I believe is not nearly as unique now as it might have been back then. At the time it was legitimately difficult to find trans femme novels. Books like *Manhunt* and *A Dream of a Woman* were still years off. Torrey Peters, who is an influence on this book, had not yet published *Detransition Baby*, and instead her work was still self-published in a series of small little books (which recently were re-published as part of *Stag Dance*). Beyond Peters' work, there was of course *Nevada*, *Fierce Femmes and Notorious Liars* and a few other novels beginning to emerge such as my personal favourite *Small Beauty* by Jia Qing Wilson-Yang. The scene felt burgeoning, and I was eager to be part of it. No one, as far as I knew, had yet attempted to talk about the awkwardness of not wanting to be overly feminine while still discovering oneself as a trans woman. This is still somewhat underdiscussed, so I hope that this book will at least help serve that niche and allow some people to feel seen.

I will not waste too much of your time talking about my influences, they are fairly self-evident throughout the story. I will briefly say that I am deeply in love with modernist writers from Hemingway (from whom I borrow a certain amount of speaker ambiguity in my dialogue) to Gertrude Stein, including John Dos Passos (his early work), Stefan Zweig, and Mary McCarthy. I am also deeply indebted to Jewish comedy and every now and again you might see Mel Brooks, Mordecai Richler, or Noah Baumbach pop up. It will come as no surprise to those of you who know my other work, that I am also deeply influenced by manga and anime. At the time of writing, I was convinced that trans women (and western media in general) needed to adopt and produce our own Slice of Life content. This is an attempt at just that. Lastly. I had the pleasure and privilege to be mentored by the great Canadian poet Phil Hall, and the exceptionally touching novelist Nancy Richler. Their insights and editing over the years, while not directly applicable to this text, made my writing what it is today.

This book is divided into five parts. The first three parts are a narrative. The fourth part is supplemental poetry, provided to add further flavour to the text, like a nice wine paring. What discontinuities exist between the poetry and the prose will perhaps remind the reader that the prose is highly fictitious—the poems drawn admittedly directly from my life. The fifth part is a little impassioned essay I wrote around the same time I wrote the rest of this book. I had completely forgotten about it until my friend Ding found it online a few months ago and sang its praises. As for parts one through 3, I have decided against breaking the text up into traditional chapters. Instead, the only breaks are the breaks between the parts. Chapters felt too constraining, as if they demanded certain things of what would be in them. I felt that my writing would be worse if I was trying to keep to a chapter structure, as ultimately, I would write too much or too little depending on what I thought it needed as a chapter, rather than what the story needed. I leave it up to you if that was the correct choice.

Thank you very much for taking a chance and devoting your time to this little book. I hope it brough you joy, and if it meant something to you, if it became the sort of book you carried around with you, drop me a line on Instagram and let me know.

With love,

@autogyniphiles_anonymous

She did long before we did.
  – *The Mountain Goats, Jenny III*

His life was not confining and the delight he took in this
observation could not be explained by its suggestion of escape.
  – *John Cheever, The Swimmer*

Part One:
Swimming Forward

An oversized reproduction of Seurat's *Bathers at Asnières* clung to the wall above the line of blue washing machines. They were the colour of the painting's river. The wall opposite the painting had once been the colour of the painting's river. Now it stood faded, yellowed, and full of small little cracks. Naomi's machine whizzed and whirled in front of her, the way old machines do. The painting, although blown up to garish proportions, was still beautiful. The two young boys swam thoughtlessly, the older boy hunched in the centre of the frame, painted darker than the others as though his thoughts kept the sun from him, the elders relaxed in the grass upon the shore—it had been two years since Naomi had been that. It had been two years since Naomi swam or moped boyishly or let herself relax publicly. In the painting the smokestacks' plume hung above the elder boy's head, promising him a mechanical end to his relaxation. The washing machine gurgled and spat detergent in upon itself. One of the florescent lights flickered. Naomi turned back to her book.

Trans people don't swim. Naomi had known the stereotype long before she started popping estradiol. She had just never once thought it might apply to her. She had presumed, in all flavours of wrongness, that it was dysphoria that kept trans people out of the water, that they couldn't stand the way they looked in swimsuits. She had not, back then, considered fear of other bathers. She had not thought about how silly she might look with her half-formed breasts in a bikini top that she barely needed. Perhaps she didn't need one- could she get away with going to the beach in boy-wear? Probably not. As it turned out, there were a lot of logical and logistical reasons that kept her from the beach, and each one stripped her of the superiority she had felt when she had resolutely promised to never stop swimming. The washing machine rocked uncomfortably.

Naomi gave up on reading again. She couldn't tell if she was dissociating or too much here, but it was one of them, and she had read the same sentence twenty times now. She returned to the painting and its smokestacks. They were a fine ideological point, but she resented them nonetheless. Couldn't Seurat have given her a simple painting of peace, of relaxation. Did he really have to include the reminder of industry, of work? Maybe this feeling was why so many of the more affluent trans girls became lost in their Contrapoints-rendition of rococo, George III, 1950s housewifism aesthetic. Naomi had always wanted to be, had always been, a tomboy. But she liked this more and more, this new ability to stop thinking, to almost stop being, and she understood now how some girls could come to fetishize it.

She hadn't even known the word dissociation until about a year before transition, when her girlfriend Susan explained to her the problem with their sex life. Naomi had known it wasn't great; she had of course presumed it was her own fault. She had always

4

been more interested in the dynamics at play in sex than the sex itself. But no, her girlfriend had explained that it wasn't Naomi's fault at all, but that she kept dissociating and that she always dissociated during sex. They would work on it together, and by the end of their relationship, by the time she couldn't sleep with her girlfriend without dissociating herself, her girlfriend didn't dissociate one bit. She had begged her girlfriend to try the inventive solutions she had come up with to keep their sex life alive: strap-ons, third parties, letting her wear a bra during it all, but it was never agreed to. Her girlfriend said no. Then she left. The washing machine churned into a new spin cycle.

N aomi lay on her side, with her head resting slightly above Claudine's left breast. Bathed in specially-bought red light the two affectionately recovered from the pageantry that often composes t4t sex. She watched as much, as much as one can watch through their peripheral vision, as Claudine's untouchable cock began to finally relax itself. She gave a little squeeze and lifted her head enough to embed a kiss lightly into Claudine's collar bone before returning to her resting place.

"This is good."

"I'm glad I could be pleasing for you."

"Of course."

"That's all I want."

"Good girl."

Despite having more than a year of HRT on her, and being in all ways a more advanced tranny, it was Claudine Withers who spoke the submissive lines. Naomi did not understand. She knew her role well, she'd been an effective femme domme long before she transitioned, long before she realized that what she was doing was not at all how a man would handle such power. But some things she didn't understand. She didn't understand how Claudine had come to be hers.

She had met her through mutual engagement in the student branch of the NDP and had stumbled through months of awe-filled interactions with her before successfully making it clear that she was like her, that she was a she. The worst interaction was the first. At an NDP bar night, they had enjoyed a couple rounds of drinks and spirited discussion about the direction the party was headed before Naomi got up the nerve to ask Claudine's pronouns. Naomi knew Claudine was trans. She knew she was a trans girl. The asking was instead a haphazardly-devised plot to be asked her own pronouns in turn. It did not work.

"You know I really hate that. You wouldn't ask a cis girl her pronouns. You wouldn't ask Frankie or Jack theirs. So why exactly can't you presume mine? It's not polite. It's not cute. And it's especially not rad. Just presume mine like you'd presume everyone else's. Or is this presentation not femme enough for you?"

Naomi instantly retreated into herself. She still cringed when she remembered the exchange. Even laying on her breast she cringed. After that exchange she had been convinced that Claudine hated her and avoided her and the NDP for months. Maybe she had hated her. But Naomi now suspected that that was just how Claudine was with people: a little terse, a little unreadable, in a way that came off too commonly as unkind. It made little sense to Naomi how Claudine had managed to make herself electable, how she'd mobilized a little volunteer army that led to a soaring victory. Maybe the terse attitude helped. After all, who wouldn't take orders from her. Why then, was it

Naomi who had been cooing orders at her all night. Why was it Claudine who had been cowed and shaking at Naomi's feet? Surely these things should have been reversed. For god's sake, Claudine was a nationally known trans activist. Meanwhile Naomi was no one, barely even a girl.

Naomi knew why. Naomi knew the power came from the thin black tie she'd worn over the shoplifted white button-up Club Monaco blouse, the assertive wide and bold black and white pinstripes on her pants. She knew there was a hunger in her eyes that she couldn't hide, and a Disney villain walk that made Claudine shake. Naomi had been doing this for years. With cis girls, when she thought she was a cis guy.

She would date a girl, one with short hair and an 'artsy' look, who would be interested in her as some sort of self-destructive art-bro archetype. Then she would domme her with a slow, calculated patience. They all loved her precision, her deep and undivided attention to how *they* felt, how *they* reacted. The less emphasis on her body the better. Keep it on them, on their emotions, on their pleasure. Make it great. Then, somewhere between three months and two years in, they would realize they were probably a lesbian and leave Naomi. That was how it went. It was reliable, like the bar down the street, like the pitcher she would drink to herself afterwards, like the poutine that kept the beer down, or the workout routine she used to convince herself that if she couldn't be a girl, at least she could make herself a hot guy.

Claudine turned on her side, her Kool-Aid dyed dyke cut glimmering as it caught moonlight blown through the window. She began to kiss Naomi with a passion. She whispered 'thank you' 'thank you' each time she stopped to catch her breath, and Naomi looked down upon herself, her less-progressed trans body, and managed a smile. Naomi did not understand, but god. God, god was she happy someone finally saw a tomboy, not a boy.

I t is 2003, the Iraq War has just started, and Naomi's family is sitting scrunched together on a Florida motel room bed. Her father had scrounged enough cash together for a tropical family vacation, provided the vacation took five days, two of which to be spent driving through the night in his 1991 silver Honda Civic hatchback with its broken cassette player and busted radio. He had buzzed his hair off so that combined with his muscular frame, he could get a military discount for the motel room. His other big expense for the year was a Walmart-brand portable DVD player, around which the family was huddled. It was intended to keep his 'son' entertained on the 23-hour non-stop drive, but the rain quickly rendered it the family's sole entertainment source.

So, there she was, 7 years old with plump cheeks and long hair, leaning upon her dad and step-mom watching the Beverly Hillbillies on a 7" screen. And then there she was Ellie May Clampett: pinning her boy cousin in a wrestling match, using her newly acquired bra as a slingshot, climbing a tree so tall that her father dared not climb after her, and out-boying any boy while still looking like TV's answer to Dolly Parton. Naomi loved her. At first Naomi thought it was a crush; after all, little boys were supposed to get crushes. Later, much later, she'd learn to call this jealous-trans-love-rage, a unique mix of attraction and jealousy trans women often hold to other trans women they are attracted to. At least that's what Claudine called it. But at age 7 all Naomi could figure out is that was what she wanted to be, a tomboy. Her stepmom had used the term on Ellie May, and Naomi had instantly loved it. It was perfect, a unique glowing term for all that she was. Except she wasn't.

She was, as far as anyone, including herself, was concerned, a boy. On the screen Jed, the patriarch of the family, knelt beside Ellie, apologizing for raising her as a boy, but explaining that he knew no other way to raise her after her Ma passed. It was played heartfelt, and Naomi felt it so. The sadness in Jed's eyes, the apology for mistakenly raising her like she was not. All this made perfect sense to young Naomi. Except, of course, that Jed should now turn around and ask of Ellie to be a feminine girl; that made no sense at all. Look at what a beautiful thing Ellie had become, the girl raised as a boy and all the prettier for it. How could Jed want her to be anything else.

Naomi lay there, episode after episode, fully entrenched, deeply lovestruck. Except, each time the credits began to roll her brain would be freed to think and to worry. Can a boy be a tomboy? Is this something I can ask my parents? How do I explain it to them without it being gross, without it being sexual? They can't know their little boy wants Ellie May. They can't know how deeply and irrevocably she makes sense to me. So, Naomi laid there, and said nothing. Nothing and panic. Then the show would start again, a new episode, a new silver shinning Ellie May to be lost in.

The credits rolled again. Naomi looked out the window, at the rain drenched wall of the hotel in front of them, the one that's *actually* on the beach. Why would anyone want to be Jethro, Ellie May's 6-foot-something cousin, she thought. He was tall and stupid and wasn't pretty one bit. Oh, damn. A word Naomi had just become acquainted with. Oh damn, what if I grow up and look like that, am useless like that. Jed seemed fine, he was a wise old man, and Naomi could really only conceptualize him as a father figure. But Jethro. Jethro was an option, and Naomi squeezed her legs together, squishing her penis between, behind, her thighs; it hurt, but oh god she prayed she could just be Ellie May.

The next two years of Naomi's life were spent collecting a little mental trove of characters she identified as tomboys, girls she loved, but also wanted to be: Princess Leia, Marion Ravenwood, Violet Beauregarde, Kim Possible, Toph Beifong, and Scout from *To Kill a Mockingbird*. Each seemed perfect to Naomi in their own way. Each held that exact relationship to gender that seemed to inherently exclude Naomi. Each were girls raised like boys, or at least fit that broad thing Naomi identified as tomboy, and were decidedly, not boys raised like boys, not like poor Naomi was.

"What are you?" asked Emma, a girl Naomi had quickly identified as a futch lesbian as the party engulfed them both. After an hour or two of negotiating the party, the first party Naomi had worn makeup to, had been out at, she had tracked down Emma.

"A girl. A tomboy."

"Listen, sweetie, you can't just have your girlfriend give you a fresh face and call yourself a girl. At least put on a dress." Naomi was dressed in black men's overalls and a black lace bralette, and up until exactly five seconds ago she had been very proud of the outfit.

"Right."

"For fuck, there are twinks here more convincing than you."

"Okay, listen, sorry." Naomi backed off. She left. She didn't turn around, she just sort of backed up and hoped the thick crowd of Susan's NYE party would swallow her. Patrick, another one of

Susan's friends quickly followed once Naomi's retreat turned into a full dash through the party. He caught up with her in the cramped kitchen she had hoped to get a glass of water in.

"Don't listen to that bulldyke. She's just threatened that her butch status can't compete with a trans girl." Normally Naomi would recoil at this type of language. Normally she would have launched into a feminist rant, or at least given a tepid sarcastic response. Instead, she gave a slight nod.

"It's not your fault she's not as special as you." Patrick continued, "I mean, you can't blame her, her strap-on could never compete with the real thing." Naomi shifted uncomfortably. She had recently been fantasizing about using a strap-on, about buying a strap that didn't interfere with her dick. She'd even talked to Susan about it, who had said she could buy one, but that she wasn't sure if she would be down for having it used on her.

"You know you are special right? You know Susan's real lucky to have *trapped* a girl like you?" A nod. Okay, this was getting weird. The homophobia Naomi had written off for the sake of the comfort, but this, well, this no longer felt like comfort.

"Don't let *women* like *that* rush you, but you'll look damn pretty in a dress once you're ready."

"I don't think I want that." Naomi said, having regained enough of herself to reply, to take a stand.

"Want what?" Patrick looked confused.

"A dress. I don't think I want a dress. Maybe if one was really cutting y'know, but no, I don't think so really."

"That's ridiculous honey bunny, all sissies want dresses."

"I don't know, but I'm not a sissy. That's not my thing." And with that Naomi quickly retreated once more, cutting through the party towards the front door. She spied Susan on her dash to the door and called to her that she was just stepping out to get herself a pack of cigars.

Suddenly Bloor Street surrounded Naomi. The air was crisp and the sidewalk swaying with swaying party goers. She tramped through the mush that pre-stomping and pre-swaying had been snow. She decided to keep her word and crossed the street and walked the two blocks to the all-night convenience store where she bought a pack of the fattest, cheapest cigars they had. With a cigar lit she walked to Christie Pits Park. She had presumed it would be packed, but the cold of the Toronto new year apparently kept any outside activities from being organized. Suddenly Naomi became very aware of how she was dressed, how she looked. The now smeared makeup, the bralette sticking out the sides of her overalls, the straps only partly hidden by the straps of the overalls. Was she alone?

Quicker, much quicker, she made her way back to the crowded street scene. There no one seemed to notice, not like in the empty park, where everyone who did not appear to be there noticed. Calmer again, she returned her focus to the cigar, to the bright soft glow. She briefly considered putting it out on her forearm. She briefly remembered how good it felt to control the pain inflicted on herself, but she pushed the thought from her mind. Old bad habits, long ago kicked, she told herself. She glanced down again at the cigar. It was already half done. Fuck, she must have been inhaling the thing.

She found a brick wall to lean against, half a block from Susan's apartment, next to a schnitzel place not good enough to last the season. Students, drunks, 30-somethings beating against the societal drive to settle down, they all slipped and fell into each other as they passed. They all looked right. They looked like they were how they were supposed to be. Naomi spit on the pavement. Soon, too soon, even the thickest cigar the store had was finished. She put it out, properly, against the wall. Then she fussed up her hair and walked back into the party.

Somehow it had gotten wilder. People seemed all in a frantic haze. Emma was near the door, chatting to Susan's astrology-obsessed roommate, the one who never did the dishes. Naomi made sure to stay clear. Instead, she moved carefully, along the right wall, in search of her Susan. She had started to feel better, but she knew a few soft kisses would set the world completely proper again. The crowd buzzed around her.

Susan was not in the main room, then she was not in the kitchen either, neither of the hallways. Then Naomi tried their bedroom. There was Susan, sitting sideways on the little bench-seat she used for reading. Under her lap was Patrick, his hand on her breast, his mouth inches from hers. Naomi's blood boiled. She rushed over. She stopped, arms on her hips, inches from them.

"Just what the fuck is going on here!" Susan's drunk eyes looked up. The recognition was limelight yet befuddled. Naomi gave her meanest stare back.

"Don't worry baby, you can get some too." And with that Patrick shoved the breast-grasping hand deep down the side of Naomi's overalls, grasping her cock. It was both a squeeze and a stroke. She shook. She pushed. She pushed too meekly.

"Susan, you are coming the fuck with me, now, please Susan." Naomi grasped at her girlfriend. His hand was still scouring her cock. Susan mumbled.

"Fucking now Susan! Get the fuck off of me you bastard."

"It's okay baby, it's all okay" said Susan slurred.

"No, no no, it's not god damn fucking okay." Naomi pulled and pulled harsher and then Susan's half limp body gave way, flying at Naomi with the force of her last tug. She landed hard on her. Then Naomi tried to get her to stand. Patrick glanced at them, stood up, and then half fell out of the room.

Later Emma rushed over to Naomi, who was sitting next to a puking Susan in the bathroom.

"Naomi, I need some help. Patrick is drunk and he's fucking up the living room. We've gotten him as far as the hallway, but he won't leave." Naomi could have asked why her, but she did not. Instead, she nodded and went to follow Emma.

There was Patrick, his arms firmly holding to each side of the doorframe, refusing the force of Emma and another girl trying their best to physically push him out of the apartment.

"Patrick, buddy," Emma said, "you gotta go. We're calling the cops on you, you hear me, you need to go." She gave him another push, Naomi joined in, and he tumbled. He was out the doorway and the force propelled him about ten steps back, though he kept his footing. He lunged forward back towards the entrance. Naomi jumped forward, her right hand held high in a fist.

"Listen, buddy, I don't wanna have to do this to you." She really wanted to have to.

"I really don't, but there's no fucking way you're coming back in. Now saunter the fuck away." He lunged a few steps forward. Naomi's arm shook.

"One more step buddy, one more step." Her arm was shaking harder now. She pulled it back in anticipation. He stepped. Naomi's arm was suddenly grabbed from behind. She whipped around. Susan was holding her arm back.

"Please, don't." she said to Naomi, "Please, go home Patrick. Don't Naomi." She moved in front of Naomi.

"Go." Something snapped, Patrick walked off.

14

Aloud quick knock, like a girl running down stairs, echoed through Naomi's little apartment. It was surely Claudine. They had known each other for a few months. Naomi was still giddy every time she saw her. She wondered if that would ever go away. It was a stumbled dash to the door. She made sure to compose herself and open the door with a swing she hoped seemed graceful. Claudine stood with a bottle of red wine cradled in her right arm. She wore a pastel yellow sundress covered in symbols reminiscent of medieval manuscripts. A bright smile burst through Claudine's face and warmed the space between the two girls.

"Hey there cutie," grinned Claudine. Naomi broke a smile in return.

"Hey. Welcome!" She moved to the side and Claudine stepped up and into Naomi's private space. Naomi had not let anyone into her new apartment yet, save her parents who had helped with the move. She had not seen Claudine's apartment either. Until now they had met in coffee shops, bookstores, and NDP bar nights. Friendly spaces. Now, this stunning, confusing girl was permeating Naomi's own little, private studio apartment.

"Sorry it's such a mess!" It wasn't. Naomi had cleaned the place meticulously the day before. A little laundry was strewn around, partly to make it look lived in, partly because Naomi had not quite got around to finding a nearby laundromat.

"Ha, you should see mine."

"Please." It had slipped out, suddenly, stupidly.

"Sometime soon, if only to prove it's Hiroshima compared to this." A nervous chuckle.

Soon they were locked in discussion, the topic of debate Jia Qing Wilson-Yang's *Small Beauty*. Naomi had just finished reading it on Claudine's recommendation. It had taken all of a

15

day to read, she had been so enticed by it. A few months ago, before Susan broke up with her, Naomi had taken the TTC to Glad Day Bookstore, but despite their reputation had found her desire for trans literature thwarted by their selection. She had bought a copy of *Our Lady of the Flowers*, but it left her creeped out and awash in self-hatred. Otherwise there had not been much on the shelve, *The Danish Girl* and a few books aimed at teens. Comparatively *Small Beauty* seemed to hold within it a world she could feel akin with.

"It was all just so human! The way she wrote Sandy, and even Diane. It was just really true, and the narrator was so relatable, so much like someone you might know or be, not some romantic dramatic thing, but a real girl. Thank you. Thank you so much!"

Claudine chuckled and told her she was welcome to borrow anything from her library. The idea of a library, a bookshelf, a single shelf full of trans literature buzzed in Naomi's stomach. She had read a bunch of stuff online, but mostly kinky, confused stuff, stuff she suspected was written by girls who had not yet transitioned themselves. None of it had rung as real as the quiet, cabin-dwelling protagonist of *Small Beauty*.

Soon a movie's credits were rolling across Naomi's laptop screen, Claudine's wine bottle approaching empty. They had maintained a respectful distance through the film. A few times Naomi had felt Claudine's closeness, an arm brushing against hers, a knee rubbing a little as she adjusted her sitting position. Each time Naomi had run her best analysis of the touches' intention, or lack thereof. By the movie's end the data was still stacked against her, too ambiguous to justify a proper move. Had she been Naomi each of those touches would have been meticulously planned, but normal people do not do that. Normal people occasionally touch each other by accident.

Claudine turned to her.

"Listen. We're good friends aren't we? At least I value this at a real-good-friend level."

"Oh yes, really, I like this a lot."

"Wonderful, then let's not have anything between us. I mean, I want to tell you some stuff and then I promise I won't not tell you stuff ever again. Okay?"

"Sure!"

"I'm not interested in sex." Naomi's heart retracted. Suddenly she was deeply afraid she had been too transparent, too obviously horny. Maybe she had made Claudine uncomfortable!

"Not in the traditional sense that is," Claudine continued, "no penetration, no being pleasured, not even pleasuring. I'm absolutely atrocious at oral."

Naomi managed a nod which she hoped did not look too confused.

"Basically, I'm a big sub. Do you know what that is?"

"Oh, yeah, totally. I'm actually sorta a domme. Or at least I was a dom when I was a boy. I'm pretty sure I'm still a domme." Naomi said with relief, suddenly finding her footing in the conversation. She took a deep breath.

"So, uh, do you like kissing, or just pain?" Naomi said playfully.

"Oh, I like k-kissing". Suddenly Claudine seemed smaller, magically made petite.

"Would you like me to kiss you now?"

"Y-yes miss."

"Good." And Naomi leaned forward and pressed into her lips.

"You're stealing my style," Susan accused. Naomi looked down at herself. She was wearing a green long-sleeve t-shirt with some sort of line art on it, tucked into vintage Calvin Klein jeans, which sat high on her waist. Even though they were men's jeans, she had recently decided they were mom jeans, and therefore hip.

"Susan, these are boy clothes. This is how I've always dressed."

"No its not. When I first met you, you had your own sense of style. Now you just wear clothes like me. You'd wear mine if I let you."

"My dad bought me these jeans! And you asked me to buy the shirt to support your friend."

"But it's the way you're wearing them."

"You're the one who always tells me to tuck in my shirt."

"But high-waisted? And the sweaters you've been buying."

This argument was going to go on for another half hour, and there was no way of denying it; Naomi had borrowed a little from Susan. But they were dating, that was normal. It's not like Naomi was not constantly also trying to get Susan to show an interest in what she liked. Besides, Susan dressed like a lesbian. Naomi was trying to be a lesbian. It only made sense that she would mimic the parts of it she thought were cool. Not to mention the fact that Naomi had met Susan over two years ago. One must update their style. Naomi could not keep dressing like it was 2016. That is just how style works! Plus, as she would not bring up in this argument, Naomi was a girl now, or at least slowly trying to be one, and even if she was not out to most people yet, that did not stop her from trying out a more feminine style.

What Naomi suspected started this argument was exactly that. As they stood in the middle of Susan's room, recently dressed after a rough night of what Naomi presumed was good sex for Susan, she could not help but think that what Susan objected to was the new feminine flairs. Of course, these were flairs that on any *normal* girl would seem masculine. But, on a trans girl that until a few months ago had been dressing full-male, well, they seemed feminine, or at least Naomi's brand thereof.

Suddenly, Naomi's body wanted desperately to cry. Stupid HRT! She loved nearly everything about it but the crying. It was too transparent. But she had realized the truth of it, and that made her need to cry. Susan only thought that Naomi was being feminine because she still thought of Naomi as a boy. After all, what rock climbing, mom-jean loving, messy haired, work-out enthusiast girl would be called feminine? Susan had just called her feminine the night before. How the hell, Naomi thought as she felt her sports bra hug her non-existent chest comfortingly, am I too feminine. What the fuck does Susan think feminine is?

Susan thought femininity was herself. Or at least she thought it included herself. Sure, she called her fashion butch once, but she considered herself feminine nonetheless. She had gone on a few rants to Naomi about how femininity should not be reserved for girls who liked pink dresses and soft make up, who spoke quietly and seemed demure. No, according to Susan she was feminine too, with her assertive, near accusatory speaking patterns, and her black turtlenecks and baggy jeans. Feminism, to Susan, was about expanding the role of women, and therefore the role of femininity.

That should have been a warning sign to Naomi that Susan had little interest or patience for gender. Honestly, it was. It was a warning sign that Naomi saw and ignored, just like all the other ones, just like when she batted away Susan's newfound "sex-work critical" perspective as nothing more than an academic disagreement. Still, Naomi thought angrily, how could I be so stupid as to let Susan equate femininity with womanhood? It made no sense! The terms functioned so differently to Naomi that she could barely comprehend the argument.

To Naomi femininity was a style of being that had once been equated with womanhood, and still was, but less so. Sure, back in the day how feminine a woman was the same as how much of a woman she was, but no living lesbian could still believe that could they? If feminine was to be expanded so as again to become synonymous with all women, then it would be meaningless. If someone looked at Naomi—if someone really knew Naomi — and then called her feminine, well how could that be? There was this famous quote that had been used by second-wave feminists to discredit Hannah Arendt's feminism, but which Naomi thought really insightful. An interviewer had asked Arendt about the difficulty of being a woman leader, and Arendt had responded that a woman should "try not to get into such a situation *if* she wants to remain feminine", adding that the "problem played no role for me personally" as "I always did what I wanted to do."

It played no role for Naomi either. She was a girl and that was enough. She had no desire to remain or become feminine. She wanted her body to feminize, and was beginning to take on a few feminine mannerisms, but fuck if she was going to grow a new personality, new interests. Certainly, she was not going to be stand being called feminine because of these few changes. The only possible way she was feminine was if she was a boy. Fuck that. She was a tomboy.

But none of this came out of Naomi. There was no great third-wave rant, no telling Susan how regressive she actually was, no quoting Arendt, Haraway, Butler, or Bettcher. There was no quoting any of Naomi's heroes. Instead, there was a meek resistance.

"Okay," Naomi said, defeat heavy in her voice, "if I'm stealing your style, change it. Dress me how I used to dress." Susan stared back at her.

"We don't have time for this, for any of this. Let's just get to the café to meet Patrick, okay."

"Okay."

N aomi was five years old and standing in the shower. She had been left alone in there and the water was pouring down soothingly on her little head. It had been a rough day at school and she was holding her junk in her hand, staring down at it all puzzled. She was about to have her first trans thought.

"If I liked boys I would just have the doctors make me a girl."

Eighteen years later Naomi would still be uncertain as to why that occurred to her younger self. She was pretty sure no one had told her doctors could do that. Nor had anyone told her about homosexuals, or dads who married other dads, or anything like that. She would later wonder if part of her five-year-old self wanted to like boys, that way she could be a girl. After all, bisexual or not, she never would become particularly enthralled with the opposite sex.

But all of that was in the future. In the moment Naomi was five and she had had a hard day. Her very best friend in the world was a girl named Livy and today her teacher had separated them. It was too cold to play outside during recess, so the girls got to play in the back of the classroom with the doll house, the colouring books, and best of all, the library. The boys, of which Naomi was apparently included, were instead ferried off to the gym for dodgeball. Naomi, had of course protested. She wasn't friends with any of the boys. They were loud, and misbehaved, and none of them could keep their arms within their personal space. It only made sense that Naomi should stay with the girls, with the girls who followed the rules and were much more fun to play dodgeball with if it came to that anyways.

Besides, the boys were stupid. All they wanted to talk about was superheroes and Naomi did not know any superheroes. She was only allowed to watch TVO, PBS, and other educational children's channels. None of them showed the scary, violent, brutish behavior she saw the boys of her class reproduce in their playfights. Brutish. She had picked up the word from an op-ed section of the CBC nightly news that her dad watched, and now it was the only thing she could think when she saw the boys' snot covered fingers thwacking each other in the yard.

Last week Ms. MacCann had used her outside voice and been real upset with one of the boys. His name was Christian and he had snuck off to the bathroom with a bunch of coloured markers in his fist. When she had caught him, he had lined up all the markers in his right hand and was peeing on them. He "didn't mean nothing" by it, he was just trying "to piss the rainbow" he told the teacher. The thought of the exercise—of the defiled markers, of his pee-covered hand, his potty mouth, his comfort with it all—it made Naomi want to crawl up deep inside her own body and not come out. How could she be expected to throw balls with such a boy?

So, Naomi was standing in the shower, promising to herself that if she ever liked a boy, she would make the doctors make her a girl. She did not know what that totally meant, but she was curious. She tried to think back to when she was even younger, when she had taken baths with Livy. She tried to remember what

Livy had. She remembered it was smoother, less snake-like, but beyond that she could not picture it. Then she tried to remember if girls looked any different on top. She knew her mom looked different, but did Livy? Was there something totally different there, or could doctors do that too? She even thought about checking her baby pictures. There must be some pictures of them bathing together. But what if she got caught? How could she explain it? She chickened out.

Instead, she pulled it back, between her legs, and squeezed them together. Then she turned her head towards the water as if to refresh herself, before looking down. Was this what Livy looked like? Could this be what she could look like? Naomi had seen the commercials on TV for all the things that made women hairless and soft and smooth and ageless, and as she ran an hand over her arms, over her legs, she thought about how her mom always called her skin "peanut butter smooth" and how she would not need any of those silly products if she wanted to be a girl. She had it all already.

Her mom had expressed an odd pride when Naomi complained about being separated from the girls and made to play dodgeball with the boys. Naomi explained that she really liked dodgeball, but that the girls were better at it anyways, and she did not want to be with the boys. She gave all sorts of reasons, about their hygiene and their violence, and her mom responded with a sort of 'not my boy, my boy's better' pride that Naomi just presumed must be right. That was what the difference was. Naomi was simply a better boy. But now she was standing with her privates squeezed behind her legs and thinking about doctors. She was thinking about doctors and smooth skin. Suddenly she was afraid that she might like boys.

"**I**magine liking boys, and, like, not liking this. One shudders at the thought," said Naomi, once again nestled in Claudine's breasts. Claudine gave out a chuckle, the type she did when Naomi's baby-tran status was showing through. Naomi blushed.

"Y'know what I mean. Stop being jaded and admit this is wonderful."

"Is that an order?" teased Claudine.

"It's wonderful and you know it."

"Maybe."

"You're just trying to get me to domme you."

"Maybe." A smile.

"Oh my god. I know what you're doing."

"Big scary domme can't take a little teasing?"

"Oh for fucks sake." Naomi rolled over so that she was straddling Claudine. Her arm rested softly on the wide-eyed girl's throat.

"Is this what you wanted?" She asked with just a hint of venom.

A smile. Naomi's hand pushed in harder.

"I said, is this what you wanted?"

"Yes miss."

"Well you're not gonna get it." Naomi's hand came off the throat and she said, "After all, what sort of domme would I be if I let the sub influence my actions."

"Yes miss."

"Yes miss, yes miss." Naomi parroted.

"Coffee?"

"Yes please."

"Dommes don't say please."

"This one does."

Naomi slapped Claudine's ass as she bounded up. Then she stretched out on the bed and listened to the morning kitchen sounds. There was the tap, and various containers opening. Claudine let out an annoyed sigh, and then there was the coffee grinder's buzz. After there was Wilde the cat's scamper as his feed tray was filled.

"Earth to Ms. Earhart, did you get lost making coffee?"

"I'm somewhere over the pacific right now!"

"Great, any sign of a coffee island?"

"That's not even funny."

"Coffee first, then funny."

"It's coming, it's coming."

"You repeat yourself when under stress."

"Stop quoting songs."

"Never."

"Here's your damn coffee, you brain rot."

"Thanks lovely," said Naomi in the most chipper of tones.

There was a silence filled with unspoken affection as the two girls attacked their morning caffeine supply. With her free hand Naomi ran around Claudine's body lightly. She traced her collar bones and jaw line, then she played with the fingers of the other girl's free hand. It was silly and stupid and she felt seventeen, but she could not stop. After a while she looked up at Claudine quizzically.

"So, *did* you ever like boys?"

"I never cared about boys. But I did like them, or I liked what they made me feel."

"What was that?"

"Feminine. What could be more assuring of one's femininity than a boy plopped on you, promising to spoil his princess?"

"I don't know, a girl doing that?"

"The heteronormative culture that we live in…"

"Yeah, yeah, I get it. I did stuff with boys too."

Claudine laughed.

"You, you let boys dominate you?"

"What, no, of course not. I just slept with them. As equals."

"As equals?"

"Okay, sometimes I would dom…I just liked how unabashedly they were into me. I could never betray my desire that openly. Hell, as a boy even the idea of pursuing a girl seemed too debasing, too vulnerable."

"Please tell me you weren't a virgin till Susan."

"Oh no, no not at all. I never pursued, but I did flirt with everyone."

"Now that's my Naomi."

"That's your Naomi."

Susan sat on the edge of the bed, with one hand softly rested on the lump under the duvet which was Naomi. The lump was rocking back and forth. Sometimes it would stop, but when it stopped it shook. They had attempted to go to the public pool earlier. It was dark out now, but Naomi had been that lump for hours. The pool had not gone well. Naomi knew she was trans. Susan knew Naomi was trans, but Naomi had told her she did not want to transition. Naomi had said that the dysphoria was manageable and that as long as she had a partner who loved her and accepted that part of her, that she was happy being a boy. Happy enough. But now Naomi was rocking and shaking and being a lump.

Naomi knew this looked bad. Naomi knew that she was a strong stoic man who should not be a lump. Why had she been unable to handle the simple gendering of a public pool? The change rooms, the bathing suits, the differences, she had handled them all before. What had changed? The dysphoria was getting worse. That much she knew. A year ago she could have gone to the pool. A year ago she went to the pool. It was no trouble, it was fun. But now she could not, now the dysphoria intruded into her mind hourly. It was black and spikey, and it filled her brain like thick tar. The nights were the worst, the nights and parties. Right now though, she was rocking and in the dark, and Susan's hand felt nice, and she could barely tell in the blanket and in the dark just how hairy and large she was.

"What would help my love?" Susan asked, breaking the silence, breaking the silence that had only been broken for the last hour by Naomi's struggled breathing.

"I don't know. I just I don't know." And with that silence was slipped back into. Ten minutes passed.

"Do you want to try on a bralette? Like one of mine."

It took a minute but then Naomi's head peaked out from under the blanket. She did not say anything yet. But Susan took her head's appearance as a good sign.

"Do you think anything you have would fit me?"

"A bralette would. They're pretty adjustable, and there's no cup or anything".

"Do you want to try?"

"I'm not sure."

"What makes you unsure?"

"Well. Um. I guess I'm afraid it would make all these feelings worse?"

"What do you mean?"

"Well, like, what if it just accentuates the manly parts?"

"It's a bra baby."

"Yes, but I mean, what if it just functions as contrast and suddenly I'm not just a man but a *man* in a bra?"

"Do you want to give it a try? I'll be here if it goes bad."

"Can we bake cookies after?"

"We can bake cookies after."

"Okay. I'll give it a go."

After a few minutes of digging through drawers and tossing clothes Susan produced a small black lace bralette which Naomi proceeded to hold in her hand as though it were a chalice. Naomi's eyes darted between it and Susan. She imagined she must look scared. She felt scared. She felt all of the possible transformative power the little bralette held. She also, however, felt most unready for it.

"Well, are you gonna try it on?"

"Yes, I think so." Naomi tepidly placed the bralette down beside her, laying it out in preparation. Then she abashedly took off her top, a tight-fitting men's t-shirt.

"Should I take off my pants too?" Susan laughed before responding.

"Only if you want to baby." Naomi began to unbutton her jeans, before glancing at the waiting bralette. She ever so slightly shook her head, then rebuttoned her pants. She re-picked up the bra, this time holding it out for inspection.

"So, um, there's no clasp."

"You put it on over your head."

"On second thought, maybe step into it. You've less hips than shoulders." That bit stung Naomi, but she knew Susan only meant to help. Naomi did as she was told and placed the bra at her feet, pulling it up and on. Then Susan moved behind her and began to adjust her straps. Immediately the tightness upon her chest relieved Naomi. It felt perfectly right.

28

Part Two:
Treading Water

T he washing machine churned again. Naomi's eyes felt wet. They darted. It lurched back upon itself, starting a fresh, new spin cycle. Slow, simple tears rolled down Naomi's puffy cheeks softly. Claudine broke up with her three months ago. Still, she had not recovered. It had been much easier to recover as a boy, she told herself. But then, had it? And even if it had, less was at stake. Claudine had been the first woman to *truly* see Naomi as a woman. To lose that. Well. The tears rolled down. For much of her early transition Claudine was all that Naomi could see. She was her horizon, but more importantly, she was her affirmation. Now she was gone.

Now she was gone, and all that Naomi was afraid of was that she would appear. The tears were sadness, but the darting eyes were fear. Every time Naomi stepped into a store, a coffee shop, this damned laundromat that she knew Claudine frequented, Naomi's eyes began to dart. Naomi did not understand. At first, she thought that maybe this is just what lesbian breakups are.

Maybe lesbians breakups are: saying you'll be together for years, then one of you going off your Spiro for surgery and suddenly treating the other like a slimy thing, then the other's eyes darting for months. Probably not. That does not sound very much like the standard breakup. As far as Naomi could tell the standard lesbian breakup involves at least one U-Haul and a lot of codependency. Instead, Naomi's eyes darted.

The missing, the longing, the abandonment, that all explained the tears. But Naomi was beginning to obsess over her own darting eyes. They couldn't focus on the tranquil painted bathers or the washing machine's white noise churn. They just kept darting, and she kept looking for her. She wished they were giant, lookout eyes the size of a billboard, seeing over the city, keeping her safe. Instead, they were small and trapped in her skull. She kept looking for her and she kept running it over in her mind why she was. Her eyes never searched for Susan, Jules, Jessica, or Lucy. She had never been afraid to see an ex before. Okay. Maybe she'd been a little nervous or uncomfortable at the prospect. Certainly, she rather dreaded a reunion with Susan, but she had never been *actually* afraid. No, the fear was new. The fear was new except perhaps for a month or two, some years back. But then that fear had been of Patrick, who was now far away safely cloistered at some west coast film school where he was those girls' problem now. He was either those girls' problem or dead in some needle-floored alley. Whatever the case, Naomi's eyes had stopped darting for him long before he moved out there.

Patrick she could explain. Those stoned red-water eyes and his grabby hands. Naomi knew what damage he did. Claudine she could not. All she knew was that Claudine had gotten weird. The daily stream of memes and messages cut to one-word replies, while the loving girl avoided each encounter with Naomi. When she was there, when they were together, the remarks were cold, blunt little slice-comments. Gone were the days of couch sitting, of couch cuddling; now Claudine took the chair. Naomi understood. Naomi tried really hard to understand. She could not imagine suddenly having testosterone back in your system after three blissful years. Claudine claimed she could smell it on herself. If Naomi was telling the truth, she could smell it on her too. So, Naomi rode the waves of Claudine's moods and jibes and nasty little nothings. She accepted that when she herself was sad she would not be consoled but sneered at from across the room. After all, it was only until the surgery. *It was only until the surgery.*

Naomi was not allowed to attend the surgery. She had offered, she wanted to be there for her love. She knew Claudine was the stubborn type who took no help from anyone if she could help it. She knew things had been strained. But this was surgery and Naomi knew about surgery. Childhood Naomi in her back brace, in her hospital gown, in her *I will never be this weak again* determination, in the chronic pain that would dog her the rest of her life, knew all about surgery. But it was useless; every little broach of the subject turned raw. At first she tried to press it, to make sure she could help, but then she realized that maybe what Claudine needed was to not think about it, in the same way Claudine needed to not touch Naomi.

They still had sex though. That was not a problem for Claudine somehow. It was becoming so for Naomi. Claudine kept acting out. At first Naomi took it as experimentation at being a 'brat', but it quickly engulfed any hope of that. No, this was a violence. They would be sitting together watching TV, then the silence would come on, the snide remarks, "do you really need subtitles, going deaf young are we?", then the silence again. Finally, usually after insisting nothing was wrong, Claudine would climb on Naomi, little domme slaps back and forth against her cheeks, then more sneering, and her knee digging into Naomi's palm.

Most of the time it was fine. It was behaviour within and around Naomi's soft limits, and while not a masochist Naomi *had* been attempting to see if subbing was something she might like. She might like it, maybe, but she was pretty sure she did not like this. Did Claudine even like this? It was damn hard to tell. Naomi suspected not. Claudine was a sub through and through. It was all about pain and service to her. She did not even like her cock being touched, so why was Naomi suddenly gagging on it? But it was fine. It was all around Naomi's soft limits.

Naomi had four hard limits: no age play, no piss play, no scat play, and *never* shove a hand down her pants. It was simple, and Naomi prided herself on the simplicity. I mean, there was other stuff not to be done, but when you are designing your list of hard limits you go for the common ones you hate. You do not bother spending hours wondering about chainsaw or slime fetishists. If you're into something *that* obscure it really is on you to bring that up. Anyways, Claudine had never crossed any of those hard limits, and when she'd been in the grey on the soft ones, well, she was damn apologetic after. She knew and she apologized, and the aftercare was there. As Claudine's self-isolation got worse Naomi almost hoped for a boundary contestation. She craved the aftercare.

At home, at her father's house, Naomi stood quietly at the top of the stairs. It was still weird to wear a dress in his home. She proceeded down the stairs, met by the stares of oil-painted portraits of beautiful women, a sign of her father's late in life comeuppance. He was now somehow a member of the middle class. The real middle class, not like how he had once pridefully claimed to be. He could now afford art on his walls, beautiful art of beautiful women. For Naomi they were each a fresh girl to compare to. Her Dad sat scrunched up, his face scrunched up in his iPhone's rendition of the New York Times.

"How can the Americans be so stupid? They'll exchange one war criminal for another for another for president!"

"Their electoral system is broken."

"Still, you'd think at least the damned DNC could save their own ass, choose a man with a functional brain."

"Morning to you too Dad."

"Ha, sorry Naomi, good point. The kettle's freshly boiled. Would you prefer coffee?"

"Gorgeous, is there any coffee left?"

"Yep! Does Ste...Naomi want some?" a soft voice called.

"No worries, I'll just have the tea!"

"The kettle is freshly boiled!"

"Dad said!"

Naomi's stepmom stepped into the living room.

"Oh that's such a pretty dress Naomi, it suits you!"

"Thanks, I like how it's sorta a sweater material. Knit I suppose."

"It's so nice to see you embracing dresses."

"Well, I'll probably be back in my blown-out jeans tomorrow, so don't get too too used to it."

"How come?" Her brow furrowed.

"I suppose I'm just not that feminine a woman. You live in your jeans too." Naomi said to the ex-body builder. Her stepmom's brow relaxed after a moment.

"Yes, that's right." She said mostly to herself.

"I just don't see why a trans woman has to be more feminine than the average woman. It would be a little insulting to cis women wouldn't it, if all trans women went around done up like Don Draper's wives."

"Yes, I suppose so."

"But you are being careful, right? No more walking at night in empty parks?" her father chimed in.

"Yes Dad, I promise I'm well aware I'm a trans woman." Naomi said happily enough.

"I think any father would worry about his daughter." Joy flooded through Naomi, as it did each of the three times she has heard her father refer to her as his daughter. She could think of nothing better from him. Suddenly, the dress felt a little more comfortable.

"Thank you." It was a simple thing to say, but so is 'daughter'. Besides, Naomi was grinning.

Since Claudine and Naomi had broken up Naomi had begun a tentative but determined effort to meet more trans women. Edith was Naomi's new favourite shopping partner. She was two years farther along to the day in her transition than Naomi, and her femininity radiated off her. She felt safe and secure and she understood the sort of clothes Naomi was interested in. She understood that Naomi did not want the sexy dresses or the floral patterns that so often comprised a young trans girl's wardrobe. Yes, despite Edith's own soft and inviting style, she knew Naomi and Naomi's type and had up until this point been quite adept at detecting it.

Plus, Naomi liked to use Edith as a smokescreen, if the two were standing in the women's section together Naomi could easily pretend they were shopping for Edith, not the boyish gender-fuck that stood beside her. HRT might have been working pretty damn well for Naomi, but her soft butch style never ceased to make misgendering a constant concern. They had gone shopping three or four times before, each time with more success than the last. They had it down to a science. The two would look through the women's section, making suggestions to each other. Whenever anything hit that right combination of price-point and style Edith would take it down and drape it over her own forearm. Then, once they both had three or four items, they would make their way towards the changerooms. Their go-to store had changerooms that split into the men's and the women's once already inside and were unattended. At the entrance Edith would hand over the selection meant for Naomi, and then Naomi would make a b-line for the men's changeroom. This was usually met with some minor protest from Edith who felt rather bad about Naomi's awkwardness and would thus try and get Naomi into the women's. Naomi, hyper-aware of her own masculinity, would then quickly and politely refuse before cautiously entering the men's. A few minutes later, and after much hate-filled mirror-glaring Naomi would emerge with whatever she deemed acceptable and the two would proceed to payment.

Today, however, was not a fun lavish shopping trip. Edith was merely accompanying Naomi to the local department store, a brutalist The Bay in a dying mall, to buy a few cheap t-shirts before they met up with some other trans gals for dinner. Naomi's underpaying soul-crushing office job ensured she had plenty of work clothes, but she still found herself in boy clothes on the weekends. Boy shirts were fine, but Naomi's new breasts made her feel confident, and she wanted something tight enough that they weren't completely obscured in cotton. The store was old and massive; built in the 60s it hung heavy with the sense of glamour long since passed.

There were two floors. The main floor was the women's, the second the men's. This came as a slight surprise to Naomi, but it did not bother her much as she knew if confronted she could still claim that she was shopping with her girlfriend or for her girlfriend or whatever. The point was there was still plausible deniability. Naomi darted around the store as was her shopping style: never systematic, drawn to whatever caught her eye, quick enough to not draw attention via lingering. Edith kept up diligently behind her. Soon she found a rack of tight-fitting, neutrally-coloured T-shirts on sale for twelve dollars each. She grabbed a navy blue and a mauve one, both size S.

Now was the hardest part, finding a changeroom. After a few minutes of looking around one appeared a few feet behind one of the several cash registers plopped throughout the store. Naomi looked at it. There was not sign on it indicating a gender. She glanced around to see if there was any nearby menswear. There was not. But she did notice that the escalator down from the men's floor ejected its riders right in front of the changeroom. She looked down at herself, she was in mom jeans, a shirt she had never returned to Claudine, and a pretty neutral-looking windbreaker. Naomi looked to Edith.

"I don't know if it's a gender neutral changeroom."

"Do you want me to go in, scope it out for you?"

"Would you?"

"Of course, I'll be right back." Naomi waited awkwardly. After a minute Edith returned.

"I couldn't tell. There's no signs and it's full of women. Do you want to try it?" Naomi took one more glance down at herself.

"Okay, let's give it a go." The two proceeded carefully into the changeroom. Naomi walked into the door, and then proceeded to turn the corner towards the hallway of stalls. Suddenly, a firm-looking woman half Naomi's size and twice her age stepped swiftly in front of her. She instantly reminded Naomi of her old high school's guidance counselor, a horrid old bat who always advised the black kids not to pursue college.

"Are you going to try those on for yourself?"

"Yeah. Two T-shirts." Naomi's voice dropped down an octave in defence. A quick mental flash reminded her that that does not work anymore. She should have gone up.

"Well you can't try them on here." Naomi's eye darted towards Edith.

"Oh."

"This is the women's room."

"Oh, I'm sorry about that. I didn't see a sign. Where is the men's?"

"It's on the second floor, go up the escalator and it's on your right."

"Right. Thanks."

Naomi swiftly turned and found the quickest aisle towards an exit. She was speed walking like a Christian soccer mom on a Saturday morning after an extra-large Starbucks. The shirts, crumped into a ball, flew through the air and smacked off the back of a mannequin as she walked. Edith looked concerned. She struggled to keep pace.

"You don't want them anymore?"

"No, not really."

"That's okay."

"Yeah."

"You want to leave?"

"Yeah."

"I'm so sorry Naomi."

"It's fine."

The two of them got into Naomi's car and she turned the music up real loud. The traffic was heavy and that hurt because it meant Naomi had to drive the limit. It would have felt so good to rev the little car's engine all down the boulevard. Instead, she drove safe and restrained as King Crimson blasted and Edith muttered about the "bitch" they had just encountered. It felt good hearing Edith's anger. Naomi did not quite feel she herself had the right to be angry. She felt too boyish, she felt like the clerk had been right. It was not her space, not yet. She knew it was her space, but she did not feel it. So the anger radiating from Edith, her certainty that it had been transphobia, and not a woman honestly trying to correct Naomi, all of that was very comforting.

N aomi lay in bed, topless, but in her favourite pair of high-waisted, vintage, men's Calvin Klein jeans. She was half-asleep after a long shift and the setting sun warmed her face. Claudine's cat nuzzled its head against Naomi's own. Smells of garlic and oregano slid through the crack under the door from the kitchen and into Naomi's half-slumber. The blanket beneath her was white and so fluffy it might have counted as an afront to God. It tickled at the lazed girl's cheeks. The bedroom window was open, a light breeze came in. Naomi had no thoughts, just bliss, bliss and exhaustion.

Suddenly Claudine was on top of her. She must have drifted off. Naomi's hands were pinned, her legs still somewhat free. Claudine's face was only a few inches from her own and looked at her in a state of faux bemusement.

"Did my puppet fall asleep?" A light slap.

"Yes Miss, I was just so comfy." Naomi played along.

"Well I've been cooking all evening for you cute stuff. Let's see if we can wake you up a bit." A smirk, nails run down Naomi's chest. *Not a masochist*, Naomi thought.

"I'm awake miss, I'm awake. Is dinner ready?"

"Almost puppet."

Naomi gave a smile. "Can you just wake me up when it's done?"

"How about we rouse you now."

Claudine's free arm slithered down Naomi's pants.

Electrics. Blood. Pounding. Screaming. No, no sound. No sound came out of Naomi's mouth. It is not screaming if no sound comes out. She had broken out of Claudine's grasp. Bolt upright. Claudine tossed aside. There was no blood, the blood had been a lie. Where was she. Claudine's bedroom. The cat peering out behind the door. *Shaking. Eyes Darting.* Claudine rubbing her back, fallen on the floor. *How. Shaking. Crying.* "What the fuck" whimpered. Bed, lamp, table, walls. *Looking around.* Four walls. Green. Picture frames. Claudine getting up. *Shaking.*

"Oh sweetie. I'm so sorry, I didn't, I just wanted you to wake up. Come here, I'm so so sorry. Yeah, that's right, rest in my shoulder. Good. You're doing really good there love. You're such a good girl. You're doing so good."

"It's okay. I'm okay." Naomi's voice didn't break. She stayed in Claudine's arms, but her voice was strong. It proved she was okay.

"I know you didn't mean it."

"I just got carried away, I'm so sorry."

"It's okay."

Claudine started crying. Then, after a moment, "Am I a bad person?"

"What? Oh no, sweetheart" Naomi sat up and began to hold Claudine, "Oh no sweetheart you're not bad in the slightest. It was a mistake. I understand. I love you. I really love you."

For Christmas Naomi had asked for clothes. Well, more accurately, her parents kept insisting that she receive a Christmas gift, and after a few months on it, Naomi had decided the nicest gift would be approval. So, Naomi asked her parents to pick out some clothes for her. Clothes were always a welcome gift from her parents when she lived as a boy. Her father, though now into his 60s, remained remarkably up on the current trends, and she could always trust his good eye for both bargain and style. She did not want to lose their shopping trips together, and hoped he was comparable in women's wear. Plus, the idea of receiving women's clothes, from her parents, as a gift—that felt like the sort of affirmation many trans girls could only dream of.

For so much of the past few years women's clothes had been a secret. Okay, Naomi had never been a sissy with some elaborate wardrobe out of place anywhere but Vegas in the sixties, but there was a pair of leggings, a bra, a sweater androgynous enough that people presumed it from the men's section. These little treasured items that Naomi early in and before her transition had clung to were normal items, but they were normal items rendered completely perverted to the common eye by who, or what, their owner was. Clothes from a girl's parents, now there's propriety! How could Naomi ever be called a 'dirty tranny' in clothes bought as Christmas presents from her parents? Even if she was called something while in them, how could that touch her wrapped in her parental approval? It was inclusion at its height. That is what Naomi thought as she daydreamed about her presents.

When Christmas day arrived two presents for Naomi lay under the plastic and tinsel tree. The tree, a family heirloom, was from the 60s and made entirely of wonderfully snow white, and probably carcinogenic, plastic. It was covered in ice blue tinsel and blue bulbs which had all miraculously survived, save a few, since '63. The oldest bulbs on the tree, just two surviving, dated back to World War Two. The simple red bulbs marked the family's uncomfortable relationship with Christmas. While her stepmom's family was *actually* Catholic, Naomi and her father came from a mostly assimilated socialist Jewish family that had suddenly, fearfully, decided to celebrate Christmas in the 1940s when they first heard rumours of concentration camps. Though they were already in Canada by that time, the possibility of losing the war resulted in a quick last name change, reversed immediately after the war ended, and a half-hearted participation in Christmas. To this day the household treated Christmas with a tone of awkward obligation rather than real enthusiasm or fervour. Yes, Christmas had always been an awkward ill-fitting affair for the family. But, when the light caught those old ornaments just right, it could be pretty too. They sparkled down upon the two red-wrapped presents which Naomi knew to be hers. It was nothing if not childhood glee.

No one else was up yet. Naomi had for once wrangled her sleep schedule into something that might prove half-productive, so she put on the kettle and stared down the presents. The household was small. Christmas was not the sort of event that called the extended family together. It was a miracle they celebrated it at all. Naomi's father talked every year a little more seriously about ignoring the whole thing. The tea steeped and steamed. Naomi sat sunken in a wing chair and watched the Christmas morning Instagram stories of her friends on her phone.

Half an hour later her stepmom came down the stairs, put on the kettle for herself, and began to make small talk with Naomi. They talked about nothing, but in the way that tells each other what they really are thinking about. It was polite, and light, and Naomi felt good. After perhaps an hour and a second round of tea for them both, Naomi's father sleepily thumped down the stairs.

"Good morning. Merry Christmas." He called before him in a voice too sleepy to be mistaken for enthusiastic, but warm none the less.

"Mornin'!" Naomi chirped back. She had been doing voice-work and was ashamed how easily around family she had slipped back into her boy-voice. Today she vowed to do better.

"How'd everybody sleep?"

"Well enough, a few nightmares to be honest, but I woke up rested." Naomi's femme voice was also a fast voice, and she found herself speaking at a rate that necessitated more detail, otherwise her answers she worried seemed terse.

"Oh, are you having those again dear?" her stepmom asked.

"A little, not really sure why." She was pretty sure it was to do the tension in her relationship.

"Well keep an eye on it. Your Dad's got a good doctor if you need someone to talk to."

"I'll be fine, I promise."

"A father worries."

"Thanks Dad."

"So, breakfast?" her dad announced, letting a moment. Naomi glanced at the presents under the tree.

"Sure Dad."

Christmas breakfast was perhaps the most important meal to Naomi in existence, but this year she would have held off on it. It was a mix of cultures and traditions that her family had incorporated or always done. There were fried perogies and latkes that the whole family gathered each year to make from scratch. Sometimes donuts were included. Scrambled eggs and mash potatoes were optional but rarely forgone, and always her father opened up a bottle of real champagne to mix with some mango juice for a half-accurate mimosa. There was also something loudly quietly missing at the table, something for Naomi's stepmom, whose Antiguan family had thoroughly anglicized themselves upon immigration. In her thoughts Naomi quietly bemoaned that missing heritage and wondered what delicious Caribbean spice blends had been ripped from the family cookbook in a rush to blend in with their new white neighbours. But then it was time to eat, and wistful melancholy to be put aside. They cheersed and toasted and dug in.

Once the food had been ate and the state of the world mutually condemned, Naomi's eye once again tentatively turned to the presents. She was a little tipsy after two glasses of the mango-mimosas and a little tired too. Still, she was eager for the prospect of a new blouse or two and casually steered the conversation towards the tree. It wasn't purely just her own presents, she was also excited to see her parents open theirs. She had bought her father a new wristwatch and her stepmom a variety of luxury organic bath and shower products. So, she was excited to see them open their gifts too. It was not just about her gifts, but boy was she excited about her gifts.

The family sat around the tree, each in their respective and favourite armchair. As the youngest Naomi passed around the presents until in front of each chair rested a small pile. Most were from each other, some mailed in by distant relatives, a few remained under the tree to be retrieved and passed out to extended family at Christmas dinner.

"Why don't you go first?" invited Naomi's dad.

"Okay!" Naomi tore into the larger of the two boxes, stripping the paper in a way she had not done since childhood. She consciously slowed herself. The box top was off, then the green tissue paper that lined the inside and then the gift. It was beautiful.

Naomi stood up and held it out before her. It was a beautiful red and white plaid duster coat, with a belt she could tie to cinch her waist. Her eyes widened, she loved it. She wanted to hug it. She wanted to go try it on right now.

"It's beautiful" she said, carefully placing it back in its box.

"You should open something Dad."

"Okay, clockwise it is." He opened a polo shirt mailed to him by Naomi's grandmother. Her stepmom then opened the bath assortment Naomi had bought for her. She rushed over to hug Naomi. Then it was Naomi's turn again. But before she could begin to open it Naomi's stepmom piped up.

"Just so you know dearie there's more. We weren't quite sure your style, or what was in with women your age, so we thought your father could take you shopping on Boxing Day to check out the sales."

"Aww thanks, that will be lovely, but you didn't have to, and Dad, your taste remains impeccable."

Naomi dug into the second box. This time what was produced was a beautiful matte white shift dress with just a hint of texture to the soft fabric.

"I love it, again, I love it. You did a wonderful job". Naomi said grinning at her father.

"Thank you so much you two!"

It was three weeks after Claudine's surgery. Naomi had not seen her girlfriend in well over a month—six weeks three days to be exact. She had not really heard from her except one-worded texts for two weeks. It had not been an easy surgery, or rather, not an easy recovery. Naomi restrained from allowing herself to feel *I told you so*. She restrained herself because she needed Claudine, and she restrained herself because it might upset Claudine. Mostly she restrained herself because she really missed Claudine. But she was mad—not mad, freaked out—as she had just learned that Claudine's mother had flown in from Vancouver to take care of her when she realized she could not go it alone. Naomi had known Claudine could not go it alone for months! Naomi had offered to be there! Naomi had been ready to block two weeks off work and Claudine had flown in her damn mother to take care of her? Claudine had not even wanted to tell her mother she was getting surgery! Still, the anger was a surface. What was really there in Naomi was the need. She needed Claudine and these months she had proudly suffered through her weird mood swings and distance, and not even being allowed at the surgery, at the initial recovery stages—she patted herself on the back for them and told herself it was all going to be good now. Everything was okay again.

Except, of course, for the simple fact that everything was not okay. Naomi was driving home from work and stressed about everything; in the mental mist of the panic spurred moment, she phoned Claudine and asked if she could come over. Claudine agreed. It was a tentative agreement which reinforced that she still was not feeling recovered and needed to take things slow and steady. This was, of course, not news to Naomi who remembered previous surgeries and was more than happy to do any caring that Claudine needed. She did not get the sense that such care would be welcome, and Naomi did not understand why. Claudine had sounded less like a girl separated from her girlfriend for too long, and more like an exhausted general agreeing to a ceasefire. But Naomi needed to see her girlfriend, so she was going to go and see her girlfriend.

When she pulled up, she could see Claudine at the frosted-glass door to her apartment waiting to let her in. In that moment she appeared to Naomi as if through a contagious fog. Claudine's fair face appeared blurred through the glass, and her expression unknowable yet twisted, uncapable of communicating yet present like an alien language. Naomi was impressed that she made it easily down the stairs. She supposed that made sense for nearly a month of healing, but as Claudine had been so silent and elusive Naomi had been telling herself it was due to a slow recovery. The door swung open. Claudine was grinning wide and visibly bouncing on her heels with what Naomi took for eagerness. She waved at her. Naomi felt herself blush and wave back. It was an automatic response. She was too happy to have any non-automatic responses. The girl's face just filled her heart.

Suddenly she was at the door and Claudine was letting her pass. The door closed behind her, a loud, hard sound.

"Why are you dressed like a mom?"

This stung. Naomi had been putting a lot of effort into exploring a slightly more femme style in an attempt to pass better. She was in high-waisted black dress pants and a slightly flowy black collared blouse that combined with her light grey eyeshadow (also a new experiment) she had hoped looked intimidating. Apparently not. Naomi made a mental note to put the blouse on the backburner of her wardrobe.

"Oh, uh, it's just for the office. Trying to remind everyone there that I am in fact a woman."

"Yeah, but not a woman in her 40s."

"Yeah. You're looking healthy."

"Yeah, well, y'know it's been a month."

"I suppose so. Do I get a kiss?"

"Of course." Claudine kissed Naomi's cheek, and then Claudine turned towards the staircase. Naomi followed behind, impressed by Claudine's agility ascending the stairs. She followed her into her apartment and bent down to pet Wilde who rushed to her and became a fever of purring. Claudine took a seat at her computer desk and opened up some form of city simulator game. Apparently, it was like Cities: Skylines but for Maoist China? Naomi began to make small talk with her about whatever the hell the game was. Mostly she asked vague question and just stared longingly, happily, at Claudine.

After forty minutes it was getting hard to not feel ignored. But Naomi was committed to not feeling ignored.

"Could we watch some TV or something?" Naomi asked. Claudine spun her chair around.

"Sure thing cutie." She flicked on the TV using the remote beside her. Naomi glanced at the empty space she had left for Claudine on the couch. She waited a moment, worried that Claudine might not join her. In the final days before the surgery Claudine had flat out vocally refused Naomi's desperate attempt to get her company. She was over, and sporting a brand-new style of bob, fresh from the hairdresser, and Claudine barely looked at her. She just sat at her computer desk, engrossed in a film-noir video game, giving the same one-word responses in-person that she gave over text. Naomi had asked her to sit down with her on the couch, her voice pleading. Claudine had said no. It had scared Naomi. It still did.

This time, however, Claudine did come over. She plopped down next to Naomi with her signature lack of grace, pulled her feet up until her knees were at eye level, and rested her head on Naomi's shoulder. Again, Naomi blushed. With her free arm she tentatively reached over and rustled Claudine's hair. Claudine looked up. Her smile was overpowering. The two girlfriends stared at each for the longest moment. Once her heart recovered enough to act, Naomi breached the distance between their two lips. Claudine's lips felt rough and chapped but oh so welcome. Soon Naomi was holding her girlfriend and pressing her against her. The whole thing lasted only a few minutes but the reason it stopped was simply an overwhelming joy, a stopping joy, a we-must-sit-in-this joy.

Her chest felt tight. She looked at the girl still smiling up at her. Everything was so right. She was in love. Big hazel eyes stared up at her and promised everything to her. They were a constant hug.

"We're going to be together for years" Claudine said.

"I want that too."

"Do you feel it?"

"I feel it so much. I've never felt it before, not like this."

"Would you like to feel it again Miss?"

"Oh, very much so."

The two had sex. Or at least, the two did whatever two trans women do when one is recovering from surgery and they're both more into BDSM than traditional sex do, that they call sex. There was panting, and begging, and moaning. It involved both a lot more and a lot less movement than one might think. Some clothes stayed on. Most came off. And both girls were quickly covered in sweat and pheromones. It ended in orgasm for Claudine, her first since the surgery.

"I love you so much Miss"

"I love you too." Claudine nuzzled her way back into Naomi's arms. Naomi smiled and felt fulfilled. This was the last time Naomi would see her before Claudine broke up with her.

A cold rain began to beat down as Naomi walked the last two blocks to the pool hall her ever growing circle of trans friends were meeting at. Outside she could see Abner hunched under the awning finishing a joint. He was a cute young trans man with a full beard and those sort of rosy cheeks that look like they belong in an old-time tavern. She wondered if his Cuban grandfathers or great-grandfathers had ever tended bar. She could picture him back then. He would fit right in if he donned some swanky zoot suit and slicked his hair back. He'd look perfect behind some art deco bar while mobsters tipped him too much for drinks, but not quite enough to keep his mouth shut about what he saw them do to some girl probably named Glinda or Roxy. His outfit today, however, consisted of a pair of those horridly fashionable bowling shirts and a pair of shorts it was definitely too late in the year for. She took a drag of his joint and kissed him politely on the cheek before entering. It was a brief conversation, but she knew she would be seeing a lot of him indoors so it did not matter.

The group was mostly trans women, and for whatever reason, trans women, Naomi had noticed, could not play pool for the life of them. All that being-raised-a-boy yet almost without fail each and every one of them had the stance of someone's girlfriend giving pool her first half-hearted go. There were three exceptions in the group: Abner, a boy who therefore could not be counted;

Lydia, who Naomi suspected picked the game up during her years on the streets; and Naomi herself, who had been playing in her grandfather's basement for much of the last two decades.

Edith walked over with an enthusiastic shyness and gave Naomi a hug before she could hang up her windbreaker.

"Hey there," said Edith, holding her own hand in front of herself.

"Hey! Who all is here?"

"Well, there's me and you, and you probably already saw Abner outside. On top of that there's Siena, Titania, Sirke, Lydia, and Tai."

"God trans people have good names."

"Also, no...?"

"No sign of Claudine, no. I did see Guinevere a few days ago though, and she said she might come...just FYI."

"Oh, and by the way, Siena is using they/them pronouns now."

"Okay cool. I guess that explains the stubble?"

"No that's just Siena. They like to grow it out on occasion to fuck with their boss. God I'd love to be unionized."

"Mood."

As pints of beer were ordered and hellos and hugs exchanged Naomi began to relax into the evening. She won her first game against Lydia, but Lydia beat her easily two in a row after that, just to prove she had been holding back the first time. She switched to an easier opponent and spent most of the next game helping correct Edith's posture and grip. It was cute and it gave Naomi a chance to do that thing where the 'dude' gets real close behind the 'girl' to show her how to do the 'thing' right. Naomi was a little worried that it was a bit too dude, or too sexual, or just too much. It really was just the best way to correct her posture, but Naomi still felt the need to mumble awkwardly about it as she placed herself around Edith's body.

The next game was against Abner who was an awful flirt, but a strong pool player. Naomi managed to beat him two games in a row and felt somewhat better about her quick losses to Lydia for it. The games continued to fly by and people came and went. Pitchers went down at a rate that made Naomi wince at the idea of what her tab would look like. But overall, the little missorted bunch – everything from anarcho-punk to ex-drag queen diva was represented – began to feel a little like family.

The night ended late. Most of everyone had said their drunken goodbyes. Naomi, Abner and Edith shared the last of a joint as they watched Tai's silver bob glimmer down the street as she rode her skateboard home. The three stragglers talked about politics, Abner told them about their astrology charts, and Naomi really considered inviting them back to her place for another beer. She had not had the stomach for being alone much lately. But she did not want it to lead anywhere, and at this time of night, inviting two drunk persons to her place might be misconstrued. It certainly would not have been the first time in the local queer community that pool night ended in a lot of lube splashing about. So instead she focused on the moment; she observed how the smoke rose like vapour out of Abner's mouth, and how the sparks seemed to hover for a moment in the glint of Edith's eyes. She noticed she was shaking; a cold rain always made Naomi shake like a frightened bird. She huddled a little closer to the group and their collective ember.

Boxing day began earlier than Christmas morning had. Naomi's father was up his earliest in years, almost as early as Naomi, and he was quick as usual to rush to the kettle and start it boiling. In the past Boxing Day had often been marked by a trip to Harry Rosen. Neither of them could normally afford Harry and they exoticized the deals and the fine Italian suits. Some of Naomi's favourite 'butch' blazers were ones she and her dad had bought at Harry's over the years. They never fit right. But now on a woman they looked charmingly oversized. Whereas in the past she had just been a boy, in an ill-fitting discounted suit. Her father was up almost as early as he was during the Harry Rosen years, but he looked a little more tired. Naomi's brain made her feel guilty for a moment. She worried that this was not the bonding experience that she desperately hoped to relive, but a strained tired father doing his best to show support. She appreciated the support, and she loved him for it. She just wanted to bond too. Perhaps it was just his age; her father was now over sixty and while in remarkably good shape for it, the body was bound to slow down, and he could not take the mornings like he used to.

Two wisps of steam, rising from their respective teas, separated the two, across the table from each other. Naomi leaned slightly into hers and let the steam fog her glasses and warm her cheeks. She smiled at her father and he gave a tired smile back. Grocery store croissants were produced and eaten and Naomi's father remarked upon how they never put enough butter in them to be anything like the real thing. Naomi agreed. It made her think about travel. She had not really realized how much more complicated travel was going to become. Neither of the two talked much, but the silence was not lacking warmth. It flowed up like the tea's steam and filled all parts of Naomi, except for the parts filled by her nerves.

"What do you think about Saks? They've an outlet store a few streets over at the mall now. I bet they'll have some good deals."

"I don't really know the sort of stuff they sell for women, but yeah, let's take a look."

"What you already got, that was from Saks, I ordered it all online for you." She tried not to note that this meant they were discount, sale items. Afterall, when had she gotten so hoity toity that she expected her gifts to not be a good deal.

"Oh, well, in that case I guess I can be certain they carry nice stuff." She smiled at her father, hoping to reinforce how much she liked the gifts.

"I think I saw a sign when I drove past saying up to 80% off."

"Oh damn, that's pretty good."

"I'll give you a hundred and fifty to spend."

"Okay, but you're gonna help me pick stuff."

"I'm not sure I'll be any good."

"You'll do just fine, you've a good eye."

"Okay."

"It means a lot Dad."

The two loaded into Naomi's father's beige sedan. It was new to him but already about ten years old. Still, compared to Naomi's '97 Toyota Camry it felt like the lap of luxury. It was so well-insulated you could barely hear the engine start, and the shocks made sitting in it feel more like floating than what Naomi had come to know as driving. Inside this cushioned luxury Naomi's nerves began to build. She had not gone clothes shopping in person since that time with Edith. It was only a few months ago, so perhaps it had not been too too long, but Naomi had been buying exclusively online ever since. Online felt safe and secure and no one was about to question her womanhood, except maybe a delivery man. Delivery men could not stop you from getting what you ordered though. Hell, they did not even know what you ordered. She wished she had put on more makeup, or a skirt or a dress. Suddenly, Naomi was looking towards her father for protection. She looked towards him as a father in the way a child views a father for the first time since she was a child. He smiled at her. How much did he grasp?

She still felt strange standing in the women's section. It felt like a trespass that was bound to be shouted out. She glanced over anxiously at the other women who did not seem to take much notice of her. The neighbourhood was not polite, nor did its people really engage in respectability politics, so Naomi wondered if the lack of attention was because she was passing. It might also simply be because it was an urban neighbourhood, and big-city people do not really concern themselves with others. They probably simply did not care enough to look closely. Naomi secretly hoped that checkout would go just as easy. Perhaps Saks was fancy enough that they did not really care what you bought or who you were, as long as you bought. But the part of the city wasn't well-off. This was an outlet. Still, it was a Saks outlet. That had to count for something. She strolled through the women's section with her muscles tense and her dad in toe.

Once she began to calm down a little the two discussed what she was looking for: a pair of plain black leggings and perhaps a shirt or two. She did her best to explain to her dad that she did not want anything too frilly or girly. He probably already understood this, but Naomi felt the need to reassert her tomboy status as she shopped. It did not take too long before the two were commiserating over the garish and remarkably lacklustre leggings selection Saks had to offer. Bright burst of fuchsia and purple cutting through otherwise completely acceptable workout leggings and an alarming amount of rhinestones reminded the two of them of their pretensions towards quieter clothing. Afterwards Naomi quietly berated herself for this and reminded herself of the joy many of her friends semi-ironically took in gaudy self-bimbofication. She told herself that just because the fashion industry underproduces clothing for people like her, did not give her permission to perform a rather puritanical disgust at what the fashion industry *did* produce. In short, she had the standard inner-feminist-self-policing chat that it seemed every feminist tomboy had twice a day.

Naomi's father pulled her aside. He held up a black cotton blazer. It had that sort of ivy-league style, like a sack suit, that promised to look best worn loose.

"What do you think?"

"Oh that's so pretty."

"Will it fit you, it's a medium."

"Probably. Let's see!" Naomi had been without fail between a size 6 and an 8 in virtually every type and style of clothing she had worn as a girl. She took it from her father and began to try it on. She could not even get it on. It was so tight that her shoulders simply rejected it. She felt her tear ducts swell. The desire to cry almost overwhelmed her. The embarrassment of being too large, too manly, in front of her attempting-support father, it was almost too much.

"Oh, funny. Usually, I fit a medium no problem." Naomi said with a stoicism. Her father's face looked a little strained to her, maybe just her imagination.

"Maybe it's mis-sized."

"Yeah, or just one of those stupid designer sizes. There really is no standardization among women's stuff."

The two looked around awhile longer. Naomi did not find her leggings. However, eventually Naomi did find a very nice button-up for work and a t-shirt that promised to cling to her in all the non-dysphoric ways.

"Why don't you go try them on? I'll just be in the men's section."

"Okay! I'll let you know how it all fits!" She spoke with that forced excitement that promised everything was great.

Panic, Naomi was panicking. She talked herself through this. This wasn't the Bay, this was downtown. This was where no one cared about what you were or what you were trying on. She had makeup on, she was going to be fine. Her hair was a little longer now. She was going to be fine. HRT had had a few more months to keep working. Everything was fine, just walk. Fuck. Her legs weren't moving. Walk! Stop looking down. Look up and walk.

Naomi moved towards the changeroom. She saw immediately that it was one of those one-entrance, two-directions changerooms, the type where if you went left it meant you were a woman and right meant a dude. A sales associate stood between the two directions, presumably there as semi-security. Naomi noticed that the women who went in ahead of her were directed by the sales associate, as she had pointed them towards the women's side. Naomi could feel a bead of sweet on her forehead. She walked forward.

"To the right sir."

"Nope," Naomi managed to sputter out as she proceeded left. Her voice had squeaked.

"Oh, I'm sorry." She heard behind her. She did not look around.

Inside the changeroom stall, curtain locked firmly in place, Naomi took a moment to breath. It had happened again! But no, wait, no. It had been different this time. Naomi had stood her ground however pathetically. She took a moment to congratulate herself for that. She took a moment to appreciate the clerk's apology. Then she breathed. The clothes fit perfectly.

Outside she tracked down her Dad.

"Well?" He asked.

"We did wonderfully. The clothes look great. Thank you so much."

"It's my pleasure. Happy to help my daughter get a new wardrobe."

T he breakup was over the phone. It was not even a phone call. It was just texts. It had been weeks since that last good, that wonderful day when Naomi had visited Claudine after work. It had filled Naomi with such hope. She was sure that they would pull through, that they had been through the worst of it. Claudine was getting better, and that meant that Naomi could recover too. But that wasn't what happened. Instead, there was more silence. Claudine text Naomi a few times, sent her a few selfies. That was all. The conversations were brief and one-sided. It was like talking to a skilled bureaucrat whose only job was to prevent intimacy. I love yous went unreturned, emoji hearts went unrequited. It was almost like being ghosted except that some responses still came—sparsely, hardly, dense in their brevity.

One night Naomi broke down sobbing. She needed Claudine and she had asked when they might spend a night together. Naomi longed to spoon her girlfriend, to make her feel good again, and in return feel good again herself. Claudine had said that she was not ready yet to leave the house, nor to share a bed. But she promised, soon. A few hours later Claudine sent Naomi a selfie of her walking to the subway to venture halfway across town for a board game night. The tears flooded Naomi.

A week and a half later the breakup came. Naomi had been warned. She had seen Guinevere at a trans social a few nights ago.

Guinevere was the closest person to Claudine. Wife, caretaker, mother. Guinevere was perfectly everything no one could be. Naomi had never surpassed Guinevere. She had never tried. Instead, she had simply hoped that the perfect-not-actually-perfect girl might see in her a compatriot. In a drunken frustration after too many pool hall pitchers Naomi confided in Guinevere, she spewed it all out, about the confusion, the abandonment, the cold shoulder, the uncomfortable sex, the way Naomi felt pulled on a string by the slightest affection; she let it all fall out in front of her. Guinevere said she would speak with Claudine. Naomi agreed, she knew she could not speak it herself anymore. Talking to Claudine made Naomi feel like a Turner Classic movie left on mute.

Two days later Guinevere phoned her in a panic.

"I fucked up. I'm sorry. I explained it all, she wants to end it."

"Okay. Thank you so much for trying Guinevere. Thanks for telling me."

Anger filled Naomi. She could not believe it, that someone had told Claudine how much her isolation was hurting Naomi and that Claudine's solution was to break up. Naomi was not going to take it. Well, she was going to take it, what else could she do, but there was no way she was making it easy. There was no way she was letting this woman who had hurt her so much walk away without hearing from her about exactly how much she was hurt. Claudine owed her that much. Naomi started writing a draft of what she wanted to say. An hour later the text came.

"Hey can we meet up tomorrow?" It enraged Naomi further. All the effort she had put into suggesting, proposing, and trying to make plans and now she was just expected to be free, to go 'oh yeah sure."

"I'm busy tomorrow with Edith. We promised we'd do a self-care day together. I am free Sunday and Tuesday evening. If it's urgent let me know."

"Could we just meet up for a short chat when you're done work?"

"I work from home Fridays. The point of the day is to spend it all with Edith, doing bath bombs and face masks. She hasn't been doing well lately, neither have I, and I think we could both really benefit from it."

"Yeah no worries, let's do Monday."

"I said Sunday or Tuesday. I have D&D Monday." Somehow this felt like the last straw. Naomi was not going to let Claudine not listen to her, to just force her day on her, not for a breakup. Since nothing else had been for the past few months, this breakup was going to happen on Naomi's terms.

"But listen, while I've got your attention, I wrote a note for you." Then Naomi proceeded to copy-paste the draft she'd been working on into the chat.

"So, I get what happened, or at least I think I've got a pretty good grasp. I think you saw me going through a hard time at work, dealing with all that transphobia, and my usual seasonal depression setting in, and you were just preparing for your surgery and you decided it was best to take a little distance. It probably didn't help that while you were trying not to think about it, I was trying to be reassuring by talking about my experience with my spinal surgery, and trying to be helpful by making sure you'd prepared for it. I'm sorry about all that.

"I also think you should know that you made it worse. The instability you saw me experiencing, most of that was because I felt you pulling away without an explanation or a reason. It felt like whiplash from how tender we had become. Worse, at this point I've got a pretty long history of people close to me using me or ignoring me, withholding intimacy for power, and not acknowledging my existence as a form of punishment. My mother did it, and Susan did it. I won't go into the whole sob story. I know you get it. I remember that time you freaked out and cried, sobbed really, cause I turned my back to you in bed. So, I know you get it. I know damn well that you get it. I experienced it as whiplash, and as punishment. When you verbally refused to sit next to me on the couch, that really hurt, as did the long silences. I don't blame you, and I'm not angry with you. I get that you were looking after yourself, but, well, I'd be lying if I didn't say I don't feel damn hurt.

"But I think it's also important to understand that this experience of your distancing influenced my own actions in ways that I am sorry for. I tried too aggressively to find a way to be reassured that I was important to you, and in doing so overstepped in terms of preparing you for the surgery. I know it freaked you out, and I am truly very sorry for that behaviour. I hope this explanation helps a bit.

"I'm also not going to lie, there was a period when I did feel angry with you. I think I've over that, at very least I can do my best to be over that. Which I guess gets to the point. I'm not going to ask you to not distance yourself in the future. I know that it's one of your main coping mechanisms. And I'm a grown woman, I can take it. But please, in the future, if it's more than a few days of it, can you please drop me a message explaining that you're doing so, and that it's temporary, and that everything will be okay. Doing so would help me greatly, and I'm sure I can be a better girlfriend to you for it. I'm sorry I failed this time around. I promise I tried.

"I was going to read it to you in person, but it turns out you're a hard person to get to in person these days, at least if you're me."

"The reason I asked to meet up was to break off the romantic/sexual component of our relationship. I'm happy to be friends with you and maybe something else will resurface in time but I definitely don't want to be a source of stress. I should've communicated this earlier rather than letting this fester and I'm really sorry for that. I don't want to be intimate with you at the moment, and barring that the next best thing is being friends, at least in my view. Does that make sense?"

"Listen, I'm sorry, but I'm suddenly pretty angry and feel like I'm going to faint. I like you, a damn bunch actually. But this feels awful and like I'm being swept under the rug. You handled this real fucking poorly."

"I wish I'd talked to you sooner about this, and I'm sorry about that. I am not surprised that you're angry."

"I actively let myself be knowingly re-traumatized for well over a month in the name of giving you space to recover and grow in. It got to the point near the end of it of having fucked fantasies of being raped by you because at least that would be some form of acknowledgement. Now you're telling me that was for nothing? After all that work I just put in you're saying you won't do any for me? We can be friends. And I still like you. I probably still love you. But you don't get to walk away from this without knowing the extent of it."

"Okay, again, I'm sorry I didn't communicate this with you earlier."

"Thank you. Can I ask why when I did see you post-op you told me 'this is the happiest I've been in a long time'? That, and the other interspersed bouts of affection...they were lovely, and the dead silence that would follow really sucked."

"The results of my surgery made me, and continue to make me, really happy by alleviating a lot of dysphoria. At the same time, it was a very draining process that left me without much energy. I've never much liked communicating by text and being unable to see you in person left me with few opportunities to show affection."

"I'm confused. I thought you didn't want intimacy with me anymore."

"I don't. That is an answer to your questions about the last month. I decided this this evening, after Guinevere called me to ask if I could work out the tension between us. I realized while talking to her that I wanted to break off our relationship but that I had been avoiding talking about it. And then I messaged you asking to meet."

"Also, what do you mean by unable to see me in person? I've made myself nothing but available to you."

"I mean I was in Montreal for a week."

"Listen I've held it together and didn't make you have this conversation sooner in the name of your recovery. I wrote off a lot in the name of your recovery. I did so by telling myself all the stuff you just told me and that we'd be able to repair and do the work we needed to do once you were ready for it. So this hurts, a lot. I respect it but it fucking hurts. I hope we can be friends. I'm open to that and I hope you are too. I'm sorry if I've been harsh tonight. Thank you for answering my questions. I'm shaking too much now to hold my phone, so I am going to go. I'm sorry you don't want to do the work anymore. I will give your collar, book, and backpack to Edith to return to you."

"Okay."

"You never answered why you didn't want me anymore. I'd like to know, so I don't spend too much time wondering."

"I realized you need a lot more than I have the ability to give. If me backing away for a month to look after my health had such a dramatic impact on you and our relationship than it isn't sustainable for me."

Naomi wanted to scream that it was way more than a month, that it was more than backing away, that Claudine had violated her consent and her trust, and had treated her like utter shit. Instead, she did her best to be kind.

"While I completely understand how that is your perspective and conclusion, I would like to clarify a few things. I can more than handle you backing away. I couldn't handle it without you telling me that's what you were doing. It was the uncertainty that hurt most, mixed with the fluctuations in your levels of affection towards me which only heightened the uncertainty. Each time it felt like my wait might finally be over only for it to resume again without any explanation.

"You say I need a lot, but my needs are really basic. All I needed was for you to tell me that you needed distance and that it didn't mean anything was wrong between us. Once things began resuming all I would have needed was knowing you wanted it to. A text here and there, you not ignoring questions/statements about if we could hang out and if you wanted me. I don't need a lot of time or emotional effort. Just honesty."

"Naomi, I am really not up for reading essays."

"Okay <3 Please read it when you can."

"I read it, but I don't really want to rehash the who what when where why. I think some space would do us both some good."

"Ok."

Then it was over.

63

A bner sat across from Naomi, smoking a joint, on his apartment's roof. The two had become close friends as there was a mutual respect, and a mutual care for one another. They had even made out a few times just to prove they really were *queer friends*. Okay, well, maybe not just to prove it. Regardless, they sat across from each other reading their respective books. They glanced up from time to time for the sake of the company or to pass the joint. Abner teased Naomi that she had a habit of bogarting a joint without realizing. Mostly they just silently enjoyed the company. A light breeze filled the air; it chilled Naomi, but only so much that she knew she was looking forward to a hot cider.

"You know no one likes her, right?"

"What? Who?"

"Claudine. Okay, people like her, but not for long. People learn to stay clear."

"What do you mean?"

"Well think about it, Naomi, how many friendships has she maintained? Guinevere, that's it. Edith, sort of. Maybe you in time."

"Isn't that mostly cause of her mental health, that she can't really be that social."

"Sure, that's part of it. But's she's also just mean. When she likes you, you feel like the center of the world, but otherwise she just sorta ignores you, and you feel it when she likes someone in the room more than you...people get wise to that shit." He paused for a minute and glanced at Naomi, hoping it was sinking in. This was his attempt at a post-breakup reckoning.

"Some people who are really good at simple relationships can't properly manage more complex ones. Sometimes they don't have the emotional intelligence, but sometimes it's just that they don't care enough to bother."

"I don't think that's fair."

"Fair or not that's what she is. You can remember her however you wish, I just needed to say my piece."

"Thanks Abner. I know you mean it well."

"I mean it honestly."

"And well."

"And well." He agreed.

"Is that how you feel about her?"

"Yeah, as a trans dude she never had any interest in me, so I got to see pretty clear what it was like to be not interesting to her."

"And?"

"I don't know, it's manipulative, abusive even."

"I don't want to think of it like that. I don't want to be a victim again."

"Okay," he said sweetly. "You don't have to. I'll be here for you no matter how you think of it."

"God damn, fucking estrogen, god damn tears, I swear to fuck you start popping a little pill once a day and suddenly you're Niagara fucking Falls."

"It's okay."

"Yeah, thanks Abner. Thank you."

A buzzing rung out around the *Bathers at Asnières* and Naomi's loads of laundry were done. Her eyes ceased their restless darting and settled on the cool blue of the newly still washing machine. No one was around and the room's pastels became a comfort as Naomi pressed her face into the warm-to-the-touch clothes. She folded her clothes carefully, so that they did not become wrinkled in the hamper on the car ride home. There was a tranquillity about it and Naomi reminded herself that it was okay to feel this relaxed, that all was well. The soft heat of the ancient radiator warmed her back as she folded the clothes. She could hear the cold early-spring wind howling outside.

Once she had gathered all her clothes Naomi hoisted them up in her half-body length laundry hamper (an investment to ensure infrequent trips and large loads were possible) and penguin walked into the cold to her old Toyota. She got the hamper standing in the back seat and then set about teasing the engine into starting. It did not give her any trouble today. She cranked the radio to the indie rock station, which immediately started blasting some corporate exec's idea of indie rock, before changing it back to CBC 1, the national news and talk network. It appeared to be a poetry reading, or someone talking about poetry. It was hard to tell. Naomi only half paid attention.

> "...About suffering they were never wrong,
>
> The old Masters: how well they understood
>
> Its human position: how it takes place
>
> While someone else is eating or opening a window or just walking dully along;
>
> How, when the aged are reverently, passionately waiting
>
> For the miraculous birth, there always must be
>
> Children who did not specially want it to happen, skating
>
> On a pond at the edge of the wood:
>
> They never forgot
>
> That even the dreadful martyrdom must run its course..."

It was not a long drive home, but too long to walk. The local laundromat, The Soap Opera, the only one in Naomi's neighbourhood, had been shut down by the government three years ago for having asbestos all over the damn thing. Since then, she'd been going to the "bathers" one, which did not seem to actually have a sign other than a big faded one that simply read "Laundromat" which hung above the cracked grey parking lot and the bleak dust of the roadside.

> *"...In Breughel's Icarus, for instance: how everything turns away*
> *Quite leisurely from the disaster; the ploughman may*
> *Have heard the splash, the forsaken cry,*
> *But for him it was not an important failure; the sun shone..."*

Traffic was bad today. Naomi could not understand why as it was a miserable weekend day when no one should have been going anywhere. Still, it was so backed up that Naomi decided against her usual jump on-and-off the highway, which when she drove passed appeared bumper to bumper. Instead, she took the city route. It was a small city, but the buildings still towered in some spots. The buildings towered so much you could not really look at them anymore and instead were resigned to people-watching when stopped at a light.

> *"...Time will say nothing but I told you so*
> *Time only knows the price we have to pay;*
> *If I could tell you I would let you know..."*

So that's what Naomi did, she watched the people, their kids and their dogs. At one point she got particularly distracted by a dachshund attempting to jump for a little girl's stick. The girl squealed a little each time the dog made an ill-executed attempt. The squeals were loud enough in their half-afraid joy that Naomi could here them through her poorly insulated car, with its window that did not fully close. The girl made her smile, but she hoped that she would let the dog get the stick soon. Too much more would be cruelty. Then Naomi was around the corner and down another street. Even with this longer route she was not too far from home now.

"…Written during the Second World War, the poem acts as a vehicle for Auden's increasing sense of uncertainness and unease Yet, 'If I Could Tell You' treads the line on transforming itself into a love poem: 'I love you more than I can say'. That much is certain…"

Then she saw her. Naomi was stopped at a red light and *there* was Claudine, in a red winter coat. *Heart pounding.* Naomi stared as she walked. *Chest tight.* Then Claudine looked up.
Claudine waved.
A green light dizzy.
Naomi returned to herself a little past halfway down the next block. She pulled the car over. For some amount of time Naomi just sat there. Her head was both too light and too heavy. There was no sense input but everything was too sensory. She could not feel to scream. She felt too much. *Breathing*, focus on breathing. Big breaths, in through the nose, out through the mouth, carbon dioxide is a natural calming agent. Just focus on big deep breaths. Calm the heart. Big breaths.
Did I wave back?
Naomi could not remember much of anything other than that Claudine had waved. She was pretty sure she went to wave back, but maybe she stopped herself. It was impossible to remember. It was going to gnaw at her. Had she actually been wearing a red coat? The memory was both hyper-there and completely gone.

Only the panic remained. The panic, the wave, and the question of its return.

Naomi nodded to herself. Her head still felt a little cloudy, nothing was totally clear, but she judged herself in position enough to drive the last couple blocks home. As she pulled into the dark of her parking lot Naomi finally allowed her body the shaking and the contractions that it begged for and then exerted from her. Beyond that, she kept it together. There was no screaming, no sobbing, no running, no mad dash. She walked across the parking lot to the elevator. The button was pressed. She waited for the elevator's little ding then stepped inside. Up, slowly, to her floor, Naomi walked into her apartment. Then she darted to the bathroom. Suddenly she was vomiting into the toilet as she tried to hold her own hair out of the way. She shook.

Part Three:
Epilogue

It was summer again and Naomi had just returned from the laundromat with her bathing suit and beach towels freshly washed. As she pulled up to her apartment, she could see Edith waiting impatiently at the door. She called out to her through her open window,

"Just a second Love, just gonna park then we can be on our way."

Abner's new boyfriend, Reggie, lived only a few blocks away from Naomi. He and a small battalion of other queers rented this mid-century split-level house they could suspiciously afford. The siding was freshly painted, welcoming and warm. Somehow its big picture window managed to glow even during the day. Crocuses bloomed from their bricked-in flower beds. Naomi suspected someone's father owned it. More importantly, however, it had a pool. So, it was park the car and up the elevator of her apartment building quick as possible. Naomi left the rest of her laundry in the car, grabbing only the suit and her towel which she haphazardly shoved into the oversized purse she had told herself she would never need or buy. It bulged, already too full. She did not stop at her apartment and instead got off at ground level and bounded across the lobby, through the glass door and into the sun. It shone down radiantly, and Edith locked her into a hug/kiss combo.

"Hey dearest." Naomi said awash in the sun. A light breeze caressed her hair and the small of her back.

"Hey there." Edith said beaming at her.

"Ready to go?" Naomi asked in a teasing tone that acknowledged Edith's wait.

"Yep!"

"Good."

The two locked arms and began a casual stroll down the sidewalk. The flowers planted alongside Naomi's building were in full bloom and their red and yellow scents filled the air. Naomi pulled out her wireless headphones, plopping one pod in Edith's ear and one in her own. The two girls began, approximately in unison, to softly sing along to Janelle Monae. Reggie's house was just south along the riverside park from Naomi's apartment, so the girls turned onto the park's path. The cooling shade of the fine old trees soon became interspersed with the sun's friendly heat, and Naomi was made to stop multiple times by Edith to examine some flower or squirrel of particular interest. She did not mind.

A few weeks ago, the two had changed into their shortest skirts and hiked out to the middle of the river. It was shallow, or at least shallow enough. It was warm then too and minnows had swum past and inspected their feet, firmly planted on the glacial rock that formed the riverbed. At first they took a few selfies and watched the water, but after awhile they just stood there, soaking up the sun, locked in an unending hug, taking in the vastness of the water around them. As they walked past the river Edith asked to do it again soon. Naomi smiled and agreed.

Soon enough they were in front of the house. It stood majestic in that simplistically comfortable way that a proud old family home does. The sound of unpopular queer pop music carried on the warm wind from the backyard. Old vines worked their way down the brick façade, around the garage. Abner's tabby cat scampered through the short well-kept hedges that lined the house. The bell on its collar jingled softly. Naomi noticed some stickers dotting the window of the main door. The first sticker read "A.B.C.D. Anything But Cis Dudes", the second that caught her eye "Sometimes Anti-Social, Always Anti-Fascist". Edith pointed out a third, a holdover from another era that read "Mike Harris Is A Union Busting S.O.B." They smiled at each other, held hands, and then stepped up to the door. Naomi gave a quick knock on the brass door knocker. It was definitely one of Abner's thrifting finds.

Abner opened the door. He was wearing rainbow swimming trunks, a button-up of which the pattern was simply the word "top" repeated in various colours, and bad 1990s plastic sunglasses. Naomi and Edith exchanged a look to acknowledge that this was indeed a lot.

"Come on in. You two are looking lovely. There's punch on the picnic table in the back. Sirke mixed it though, so I might take it a little slow. She ran out of vodka and we caught her adding gin to the mix too. Um yeah, otherwise everyone's here, if you need the bathroom it's the first door on the left coming in from the pool. I'm really glad you came."

Edith blushed a little. She was never very good at being invited places. Abner rushed off to what sounded like Sirke's yell for him.

The two girls entered the warmly dark house, removing their shoes before traversing towards the shinning French doors that led to the pool. Their windows offered a glow that felt like a light to be walked towards. Naomi briefly wondered if she could glow like that. Maybe she could be a soft light that warmed her friends.

The doors parted to one of those midsummer Saturdays from which Sundays were spent in recovery. The music was louder, the colours were brighter, and friends were smattered in small groups among the carefully curated overgrowth. A crab apple tree bloomed. A Sakura tree stood proud and shaded a corner of the pool. Its long branches stooped and threatened to skim the surface of the pool. Lower bushes and leafy plants partly obscured the squirrels that darted through the scene. And still, very still, at the far corner of the untamed harmony that was the garden, a wild bunny watched half-hidden behind a fern. Everything was green and brown and beautiful. The bodies of her friends danced around, carefree and comfortable. The sun washed over and warmed the beige concrete pool deck. It glinted on the pool. Tai waved at Edith and she walked over to join the group around her, and when she passed in front, Naomi she felt full inside. She was so beautiful. Something brushed against Naomi's leg and she looked down. The tabby from before looked up with big green eyes. Naomi half-bent to pat it. It let out a short purr and then continued on its way.

Siena swam topless in the pool. She yelled out to Naomi.

"Come in dearie, the water is so warm, look my nipples aren't even pointy!" Naomi blushed.

"Okay, just uh give me a minute." She returned to the house.

A few minutes later Naomi emerged in a simple black swim-team style one-piece. She had not bothered to tuck. A bulge was okay here. She glanced around for a moment. Edith blew her a kiss from the other side of the pool. Then Naomi carefully placed down her bag and towel, walked over to the pool and stopped so that her toes were just over the edge. She dived in. The splash glittered in the air. It had not been so long since Naomi was here, but it felt good to return to the garden.

Part Four: Poems

Before I transitioned, I was a published poet, active in various parts of the Canadian poetry scene. I have not published any work since I transitioned. I am not sure why I stopped publishing. Perhaps transition gave me something that made me feel less desperately the need to be heard and known by strangers. It is with great discomfort and uncertainty that I share these following poems with you. I share them now for a few reasons. First, I am aware that this little book is just that, little, and I want to make it worthwhile to the buyer. As such, these poems are somewhat of a little extra, a buyer's bonus. Secondly, I have selected these poems out of a great many that sit around my house and on my phone because I believe they thematically complement the themes of the story. Much of the story attempts to skirt around and underemphasize the turmoil that occurs in its pages. That is the nature of the narrator. These poems do not do that. If the story is sparse, these poems are richly packed. They are the dessert after the meal. The story is fiction, whereas the poems are drawn more directly from my life. Perhaps that will satisfy those of you who are looking for me in these pages. Some of them are ones from before transition, ones I had the immense pleasure of being aided by Phil Hall's hand in editing. Others are newer. I wonder if you can tell which are which.

I hope you enjoy.

Auto Anon

My   friend

   Ana

   Has a trans stamp of salvation

A weather

       Beaten face

The last time I saw her   a kegger

   "Take this and drink it"

Later

   Cuyahoga on a bathroom floor

   I told her

       She was a genius

"Just like everybody else."

REVERSE TOMBOY

Middle-class romantic love sweeps
In, against, domestic green stillness.
Extremely Cruelly Women's experiences
Totalize my own uncertain Jack Rabbit
Conditions, primarily said with diligent
Latke eating cultivated reservation.

Pursuit not expected sourly.
Decent Christian pagan friend
Yet given the true circumstances
Gender adultery & post-wedding advocacy
Penetrate the intercourse from a blue marble
Archimedean point sparling wine
Distance.

The patriarchs of implications
Call out to us two, rendered simple
And no longer pure, for proper education.
They worry that lovers' eternity combined
With free floating knowledge will turn our
"us"
Of two, into a glorious "us" that Joins
Them, petty local gods of property.

But my stomach lining's wearing thin
And you shuffle grey when you try
To walk that highway to Damascus my dear.
The garden is no longer wild wonderful weeds, but
Now mathematically trimmed, whimsically
Filled with not a twig out of charming place hedged-animals.
And cops have once again road-blocked the pretty Apian way.

AUTO ANON

So what now is this LED chastity
Can we retreat against the chimeras
Avoiding Continence's purple infirmities?
Do we accept our bodies' sovereign preservations
Even and although they mix with the public?
Should we obey our represented weakness?
Let us give into to our lower-class prices.

Take Flight

We will be deities
When broken
Bottles assault the floor
Lesser colours
Of passion
Leap across the oil
Glass houses
Break and unbreak
When we take flight
Space programs
Shutter and halt
See my love
We will be above
On charges
There's no grasp
Only promise
One and only
Way to be
When gods
Hammer and sick all
At their door
Dogs yap and moan
Lights turn out
People flood the homes
Ruination takes hold
Nothing left
They can use
You've only one direction
To climb
The moving has come true

A Poem In Her Honour

I knew a girl who liked *it*
I do not mean sex
And I would say that she liked *it* too much
Except that that would imply a proper
Amount possible, bearable,
To say she liked *it* too much would mean
That a normal person, or more likely
An abnormal yet adjusted person like myself
Might withstand its inclusion, in a film scene
Just for a second, flashing and fluttering,
Flattened and romanticized by pervert lens.
But no. *It* is truly impossible to withstand.
I don't think anyone has ever put *it* in a film.
So I cannot say she liked *it* too much. Once,
Would have been too much. I can say she
Loved it. She squeezed *it* blue. Involving her
Pussy was insufficient, and difficult to do.
She needed *it* direct to her chest. Falling on
Her sword so the yonic wound could deliver
It to her heart, a bubonic tonic. Screaming!
But only nouns can enter you. So each pink
Velvet morning she'd rise and gracefully slink
Out for *it*. Her grey water beauty was entirely
Dependent on her proximity to *it*. If she had
Merely posted online about *it*, or only read,
She was hot custard yellow softness. If she
Had seen some, glimpsed through a window
Darkly, carried out among the city steam or
Frying electric in a farm field, then she was
Pond still, grey graphite sleep plastic beauty.
Had, however, she had some of *it*. Truly,
By most gloriously depraved fuck I swear,

Reverse Tomboy

And I only saw it twice, she was Hapsburg
Purple Sisi radiance Einspanner ordered and
Only whipped cream consumed beautiful.
I will not comment on what bones are left
Of her now. No one is dumb enough to need
A cautionary tale of *it*. So, I remember her
Grey beauty. The purple was too effulgent.

You Always Liked Black Leather

The past has his hand wrapped around my neck

And all I have to do

Is get lost

In a little   hopeless whimpered

Needle scream

Sail to Pyra

With my petrified heritage
Any my traffic jam thoughts

Let   the bay horseshoe

Wash my feet

Clean and

Discard the boots   black dog hide diamond studded

But still designed for a trench

Urchin caressed you lent them to me

Throw   Them

Into white sand or well

Sinking deep into the aeons

Of a new

Personal dawn.

No longer the black and blue objective

It   never fit my skin

I will be free.

But somewhere in the back of my mind, I will wonder
Are you are burning books once again.

REVERSE TOMBOY

Late last night   I think

I heard you calling

You

And all my bad old habits

Like a re-representation

Like a book in its third edition

You are changed for these times

And I, I do not know that

I am

Anymore more than a

Stage in your life

Walked over and said your lines upon

To applause

Gored and adored

You aging matador you

Mercy for a bull like

Like like like

An ending that ends like the tip of you tongue

AUTO ANON

Before

It is dark out

But there is noise from the street

I don't want to go over

His voice is lucky strike years

And I think I realized that my dad wouldn't

Heard the small rustling of a blanket

Dragged down the stairs

I've stories

Really far too bitter for anyone to drink

The vocabulary to talk about it

Belonged to Italo Calvino

I'm just telling you things

Have you done that

Fucking Awful

She would imagine the crowd and **tell them**

Not it.

Will be the headline front page

She sang my spine

Like Richard the Third

What decent person would

Turn his head to her like a priest

"You look lost love"

Like a parked hatchback

letting a minute

oh.

is that all.

again?

REVERSE TOMBOY

Allie has long blonde hair

And worries

That

That

Is all you need

To know.

Auto Anon

We were demolished like brutalism
That great Weberian stain
You flew international and then said you were
Clean, with a new Dawn
Like the fable of the duck and
That great oil spill

But you were not you
Just another dirty bird
And a bird on the beach
Is a fish in the sea
So be mean to me
Mean to me
One more time

REVERSE TOMBOY

Written at Shakespeare and Company

I'm a visitor here again, a fucking tourist
You got to stay, to be from here, walk in
I thought I would, we made plans, You
Made me leave. I withstood all your cuts
You could not force me away, I was purple
Red, black, blue, and swollen. I stayed until
You gave up your indirect ways, unrestrain
Now, this bookstore, old rugs, sunk shelves
You must have come back here. You must.
I am back here. A block from your favourite
Bar, The English Shop, I ordered in German.
All the books are better here. They're better
When English is foreign. A loud man brags
About his CIA, Mossad buddies. He longs
For their trauma. A calculated restraint.
I was gay here. But I didn't know it.
And your slaps couldn't convince me.

Auto Anon

I hate distance
Binary emotional physical distance.
And yet both of us have trafficked
In distant sour candy love so often
We have kept time by train wheel metronome.
We have born soul and breast to web cameras.
We have tasted and choked on bone marrow
and hid behind its clean white case.
We hate distance except for in its place.
And we move closer, yellow and smooth
It felt good, but you have felt tragic,
Asserting with tepid fear a taste for the blues.

We mark our date a month away, too soon
And do nothing to signify our children's eve.
We eat where there was before immediately
A failure, feminine and bravely rosy cheeked.
The waiters dance the cuckold's dance late.
And a sad emo boy wines about the heat.
Music, food, wine, and Moulin Rouge posterity.
We are all besides & insides & all immaturely halogen happy.
A wet sloppy puppy kiss that we clean immediately.
I worry laying siege to each other
Hoping for reassurance.

REVERSE TOMBOY

Pretty Woman Prison (GRS): Written as lyrics for a band that broke up before they could record it

From the pussy cuttin' room I see the prison
It is darker than night
And with the flowing of blood and flicks of the knife
The seducer devil man's hands gave me back my life
Oh toss it away!
Lob it away!

שְׁקֹט
Shuck it
Come here and fuck it

The prison it hangs there, heavy acknowledgement like
Then the devil man says to me
"Y'know once they're cut, I fuck em once or twice,
Just to make sure they're all used up real good n' nice"
Until they fray!
Oh get away!

And the prisoners sang:
Oh I don't mind being a girl all the time
I was born to bleed
I was born to bleed

So the devil doctor replied:
You know you can't walk away, it's time
I'll make you pay
I'll make you fray

Auto Anon

And the nurses they pounce soft, a real jaguar fright
The screams sound like moans
To Vishnu watching over the abject flesh sight
So I sigh in great relief, some company will be nice
Make me nice!
I'll pay the price!

שקט
Shuck it
Come here and fuck it

I can be cruel

I don't need an outfit for that
I don't need black goth or bimbo gloss
I don't need mouthwash
I know what I said.
Even though we're adults
And you're leaving me
The bottle and the Tylenol don't call
Like they used to.
I don't mind
I can be cruel in understated
Garb quietly
In self defense
I placed six lily flowers on the grave
I couldn't afford more
Then I consulted the Michelin Guide App
For lunch.

Buying Nike

    Oh little one
My spiritual credit card
You've drained me dry

With your bankrupt sole
Its imprint still on my cheek
Rolled
      Down
         There
red and shining
Like an Achaean fleet
On the water
On the way
       To wage
A different idea of love

The Parade

Last summer eating ice cream in the hot Vienna sun
We waited for the parade to start
And the people parted like an ocean waiting
To drown an army.

A Cinderella carriage came through
But black and red and white like bone
And on it stood a man with a ben-hur whip. Below him,
Six men and women leathered and tethered to the cart.
"Oh what fun!" you smiled.

It's alright to hate you now.

I tell myself,

It's alright to hate you now.

The Family Man

There is no narcotic
It is looked at
With unmitigated evil
Portrait with a cigarette
And their belief
Manifest nostalgia
Sprinting through the streets
For outmoded degeneration
And a nice suit.
It's a real nice suit
Fit for a Machiavellian prince
And a room locked
To his bride
Beating on the parapet
For you know you have
A wife
You can buy the house
For the rest
The car in front
Chasing you halfway round
Sweet squelches
Of recognition
But that Formica table
The family comes
Charging in

REVERSE TOMBOY

Traum-a

The depth of the ocean dark
Vacuum sealed around my bedsheets
In this howling silence a flayed face flies
What might emerge
My leg lays in no man's land, not warmed
By my body. Sheets and face shaped hole.
I allow one. Another face, the man bent standing
Down joyful eye contact with victim
It sings, "You can't move can you boo"
Maybe.
It pulls the room. In.
Reminding me. This isn't really mine.
Behind me.
That's where and when you appear.
Sense in the mirror.
Licking my reflection.
Barbed tongue against groin.
My music drowns your not-sounds.
Do you slip into my lovers
To see how I feel?
To spoon or be spooned
Will you slither into me then?
Or impatiently as before.
Like children and cats,
Demons love to play with their food.

Grey hairs and wide eyes
What a perfect, sorry little girl
You've exhumed from
The tatters of your tatters
Of your old young self.
I miss
Your electrics even
Though they've never always yet
Coursed through my
Soft flexing living dead flesh.
A hand arranges
A grasp gasps hair.
"Drink of this
For it is my body" *sarcastically*.
Eagerly I am eager, are you?
Have we killed him?

My needs reach,
Across the sameness
That is a boarder.

Reverse Tomboy

Sad Oxen Mermaid Girl

I stand up and lean forward becoming
My bike's very own figurehead
Not tumbling forward
Only trying, to work my way ahead
And I know though I'm not forsaken
I'm a fair ways too adrift
So these potholes, plot holes,
Make these streets' sunset strip.

Thus the girls, on the corners
Are dressed like for a quarter past nine,
And they tell you, they can love you,
For just a short gasp of time
Still, they'll admire your bra
All lace and tight front clasp
And the bourbon stain on your butch suit
Assures them that you're truly first class.

And you cry that gender's a moloch
An idol demanding so very much
Though the fire to him you pass
Instead of just growing up
It's belly full of sardonic laughter
But only the resistance's parents' tears
Crying from a thousand blind eyes
Filth! Ugliness and solitude!
The funeral-pile flameless now

Part Five:
Trans Femme Masculinity,
What Do We Want?

Who the fuck are trans women, and what the fuck do we want? Those two questions have come to increasingly define my own relationship to myself and my community—my trans community. The two obvious answers to this are: we are women who are trans, and what we want is to be left alone as women. Some of us medically transition, some of us don't. We are all women and we transitioned because that's what we are. Now, I am partial to this view, and I think within the community that's about as good an explanation and an answer as we can currently arrive at. But the problem comes when we leave it there for the outsiders. When we say we are women and transitioned because we were women, the white cis het dude or lass listening to our interview, reading our blog, or chatting over the watercooler does not get that it is in fact that simple. Instead, what they hear is filtered through their own conception of gender. What they hear is that we transitioned to be feminine. Worse, sometimes they hear that we transitioned because we were feminine. And, okay, there is something to that; we transitioned because we did not want to be, were not, men. But that's not the same. Aided by the past two decades of 'supportive' queer (not made by, but made about) media, the self-declared progressive, the liberally-minded suburbanite, thinks they've a pretty damn good idea of just what trans women are about. They think this without having ever heard the term trans femme. Instead, they picture Jules from Euphoria, Sophia Burset, Nia Nal, or Nomi Marks. In their defense, at least they've mostly learned to stop picturing Buffalo Bill. They probably still picture Caitlyn Jenner. Despite all this 'progress', or rather because of it, they've got a pretty good idea why you transitioned. You transitioned because deep down, in your heart of hearts, you're a girly girl. That stopped me for years.

The recent fashionability of transness (corresponding with the fashionability of drag queens) reinforces the idea that trans women are not only trans, they are extremely feminine, so much so that they must be trans. It is presumed that only the most feminine of men transition into women. That pre-transition we were all a bunch of lispy twinks who genderbent like it was nobody's business, and could do a better face than our mother by the 9th grade. Of course, the reality is often dramatically different. Most of us, I would hazard, weren't screaming queens. We were nerds. Nerd is what you get when you think you're a boy, don't want to be hyper masculine, and have that dysphoric shyness that accompanies so many of us. It's why trans girls still get together to code and game. It's why we host board game nights and DM D&D campaigns. We were mostly nerds. I was a nerd. Well, I was a nerd a little more obsessed with fashionably punk attire and hair, and a deep-seated interest in being a good and attractive lover. I'm not sure if I ever was either, but I tried. I hit the gym, a lot, and made a point of never orgasming before the girl in any porn I watched. Secretly, even to myself at first, what I did do while watching porn was mimic the girl's speed and rhythm. I told myself I was training myself to be more pleasurable, to last longer. Now, of course, I know what it was about. But the fact remains, I was a self-conscious nerd, who did things like fashion, elaborate hairstyles, and fastidious gym routines in a misguided attempt to achieve an attractiveness in the eyes of my partners that I thought unattainable to anyone but women. Others had it worse; some of the hottest trans butches I know of once appeared to the world as massive hulks of testosteronic proportions. Not all of that goes away; I mean, they're, I just said it, the hottest trans butches I know.

. . .

In Infect Your Friends and Loved Ones, Torrey Peters describes the experience of throwing a football post-transition. She describes how "The girl down at the water's edge throws the football in a beautiful spiral, so smooth and steady you could use it for a drill bit. I want to catch that football. I haven't caught a football in three years. And normally, I'd be embarrassed—I'm self-conscious about the way displays of athleticism curl my body into the old shape: arms lank, shoulders loose, hips solid and straight; shrugging off the balancing-a-book-on-my-head pose that I've cast my body into. But today is Trans Beach Pride at Seattle's Dyke-Ki-Ki Beach, so who cares? No one here is going to think I'm manly". Peters' work is beloved among trans readers, and you can see why. No made-for-cis-by-cis trans narrative is going to talk about that, about the skills we still have, the aspects that render even the most femme trans a little bit of a tomboy. That's what I always wanted to be, a tomboy. I'm not non-binary. I'm a binary trans woman, but I always wanted to be a tomboy. As a child I would sit around watching Elly May Clampett, Marion Ravenwood, Ginger from Gilligan's Island, and to a lesser extent Princess Leia and want to be them. I did not want to be them because the Disney Princesses seemed unattainable. Hell, I wanted to be Mulan too. I just knew what I was, a tomboy. I had no interest in high femininity. I wanted most of the same stuff boys wanted. I just wanted to do it as a girl. In her video "The West", high femme trans gal Natalie Wynn says "Being trans is so weird. Like you have all these childhood memories that are just totally discordant with your adult gender identity" in reference to playing Age of Empires II while growing up. I still play Age of Empires Two (the rerelease of course), so I can't say I agree with her, at least not totally, and that's the problem. For a lot of us we never wanted to be high femme, most of us still don't want it. Hell, many trans women aren't even interested in passing. Instead, it is society that is interested in us passing. Some of us tomboy trans gals femme up, I certainly did. But often it is not all the way, nor do we want it to be. Further, many of us are at least partly, if not mostly, motivated to do so to avoid being yelled at in bathrooms, and accosted on the street. Yet even in our own community there remains a pressure not to throw that football, not to let our voice drop down in anger, not to admit we've got a whole shelf of military history books at home obtaining a new layer of dust.

. . .

Ernest Hemingway was a trans woman. Or at least, if you want to get academic about it, there's a damn high chance Ernest Hemingway had gender dysphoria. In "The False Macho" John Hemingway, Ernest's grandson, writes of Ernest's complex relationship with his trans daughter, Gloria. In the article John points to several short stories such as, "A Simple Inquiry", "A Sea Change", and "Big Two-Hearted River" as well as two of Ernest's novels Islands in the Stream and The Garden of Eden to suggest a transgender Ernest Hemingway. John also retells the first time Ernest caught Gloria putting on women's attire (please note John refers to Gloria as his father and uses he/him pronouns for her): "The first time that Ernest saw my father putting on a pair of nylons was in the Finca Vigı́a. Gregory was about twelve years old and it was soon after he had won a national skeet shooting contest against adults in Havana. Ernest walked into his son's room, saw what he was doing, and walked out without saying anything. A few days later, when the two of them were alone by the swimming pool, Ernest said to my father, 'Gigi, you and I come from a very strange tribe,' and that was all. But it was more than enough for my father. He understood instantly that his father shared a secret with him and one that no one besides themselves would ever understand." Likewise, in her article "Hemingway, Literalism, and Transgender Reading" Valerie Rohy draws attention to Ernest's own attempts to feminize herself, such as taking on the name Katherin, imagining herself as a woman during intercourse, sex change fantasies, styling herself in a way she perceived as feminine, and an unrealized desire to pierce her ears. So what do we do with this information? It's readily available with a simple Google search, and yet on the increasingly long list of historical trans figures, most of whom are either less famous or more attentively trans than Hemingway,

Hemingway never makes the list. Are we ashamed that someone so famously masculine, so boorishly drunk, such a womanizer, could have been a trans woman? We shouldn't be. With some notable exceptions, it's a largely undiscussed truth that the most cringe-creating of chasers are our unrealized sisters. We see it in them, and no doubt is a small part of why we avoid them so insistently. And what of our non-passing trans sisters, the ones the worst of us used terms like 'brick' and 'mortar' to describe? These women that their fellow trans women shy away from, or rapidly denounce, just how much of that is internalized transphobia? More accurately, how much of that is the fear that we see ourselves, our masculinity, reflected in them? Trans women are masculine. At least many of us are, and many of us enjoy that we are. Trans butches and futches unite. It's time for the trans femme community to accept that among us there are dommes, and D&D nerds. There are butches, and futches, and high femmes who can fix your motorcycle for you. We are not cis women, and cis women are not all femmes. We must stop pretending either of those things are true. Don your leather, put your girlfriend's cock in a cage, and take a ride on your new yellow and black Kawasaki.

Bibliography

Hemingway, John. "Ernest Hemingway, the False Macho." *Men and Masculinities* 15, no. 4 (2012): 424-431.

Peters, Torrey. "Infect Your Friends and Loved Ones." In *Stag Dance: A Novel and Stories*. New York: Random House, 2025.

Rohy, Valerie. "Hemingway, Literalism, and Transgender Reading." *Twentieth Century Literature* 57, no. 2 (2011): 148-179.

Wynn, Natalie. "The West." Posted 13 July, 2018 by ContraPoints. YouTube. 23:31. https://www.youtube.com/watch?v=hyaftqCORT4.

www.ingramcontent.com/pod-product-compliance
Lightning Source LLC
LaVergne TN
LVHW090927060825
817840LV00022B/187